The Cadet's Threat
A Hannah Sparrow History Mystery

by

Shawn T. Shallow

For information, email Cozy Cat Press, cozycatpress@aol.com or visit our website at: www.cozycatpress.com

COZY CAT
P R E S S

ISBN: 978-1-946063-85-4
Printed in the United States of America

10 9 8 7 6 5 4 3 2 1

Dedicated to my friends in Leighton, Alabama, who so warmly welcomed a relocating Yankee.

Acknowledgements

My thanks to the Lenz family for historical background; Josh and Jennifer Harbin for naming assistance;

and the LaGrange Military Academy site volunteers for reference material.

Chapter 1
Leigh Acres

"Do you believe in ghosts?"

"Not unless you count my bloodsucker ex-husband," answered Lisa with no humor whatsoever.

"I think you're referring to vampires, which are technically the un-dead," corrected Hannah.

"Okay. Then I'd have to say no. Why do you ask?"

"It's just that I find this place spooky sometimes. Especially the old cotton mill and the empty downtown," whispered Hannah theatrically, covering her mouth as if not wanting to wake a phantom.

Hannah's oversized glasses slowly moved from the abandoned cotton mill to the empty downtown just a block away from the rural Alabama porch on which they sat. Even at dusk, you could make out her little white cottage with black shutters, and a ground level front porch bordered by two pillars on either side. It proudly displayed an engraved plaque of black with gold letters indicating its original function as the Mill Overseer House. Perched on the roof was a cupola with a weather vane depicting a country rider, which rarely moved unless rebuked by an especially strong wind.

The abandoned cotton mill and the downtown itself stood frozen in the distant past, now devoid of the people who once claimed it. The town's center was a collection of old buildings and a main street that looked like a carpet laid for a dignitary who never arrived. The empty stores were anxiously awaiting merchants at any moment. Sounds were limited to an infrequent passing car, barking dogs in distant yards, and birds. Against the back wall of one of the old stores stood a bicycle with its chain dangling on the sidewalk. One had to wonder where the rider could possibly have gone, and how many years since their departure.

Hannah pointed in the direction of the bike. "Can't you imagine some long-dead cycler trying to retrieve the bike to complete the journey he started before being so rudely interrupted by their unfortunate demise?"

"You mean like a restless soul doomed to walk the earth because of some unresolved conflict?" asked Lisa.

"Yes. I don't actually believe the restless soul bit. I'm just saying that my imagination can conjure some frightening images when things go bump in the night around here," commented Hannah with all seriousness.

"Don't think about it. Try to picture this place back in the day when it was the big stop-off on the way to Nashville," said Lisa ruefully, referring to "the day" somewhere between Prohibition and Sputnik. "Besides, Earl and I are just a shout away."

"I appreciate that. So what happened to this town anyway?" asked Hannah.

"They built the highway too far south and everybody switched to Mushoals," confirmed Lisa with a glance past the railroad track to the unseen town too far in the distance. The only people who pronounced the town's official name of "Muscle Shoals" were smartphone directional app developers.

Hannah sat back, mollified. She had come to trust Lisa in all matters from local history to the best plumber in a pinch. Hannah was a newly arrived Northerner and Lisa a lifelong Southerner. Lisa had quickly adopted the new resident when Hannah moved next door across the abandoned lot now serving as Lisa's vegetable garden. There were quite a few abandoned lots, as old homes fell into ruin over the years and were removed—often after burning. The closest neighbors now were a young couple remodeling one of the empty buildings and an old curmudgeon living upstairs from what had been the telegraph office in times gone by.

"What else did the town have to offer back in the day?" asked Hannah.

"Well, there was a hotel there," said Lisa, pointing to a vacant lot near the railroad crossing on Main Street. In Leigh Acres, everything was near Main Street—the town being about four square blocks.

"There was a restaurant across from the flower shop," Lisa continued. Hannah knew the flower shop—her house was behind it, separated by another empty lot.

"I wish it was still here," lamented Hannah. The closest food was a grocery store in Town Creek about fifteen miles down the county road.

"And, there was an old house next to you with a family of midgets," said Lisa matter-of-factly.

"Midgets?" asked Hannah again, doubting Lisa's veracity.

"Yes, retired circus folk," said Lisa with authority, indicating the point was closed.

They sat in silence, which they often did. It was warm with a slight breeze. The mosquitoes were generally at bay. Lisa had "learned" Hannah to place a dryer sheet in her upper pocket to act as a mosquito repellant. She also said to eat bananas. At least she wasn't told to wear the fruit.

Lisa sat and sipped on her sweet tea. Even in the lawn chair, her tall and slim form was evident. At forty, she was considered cute with bright blue eyes, a broad smile, and sandy blond hair, even if her skin was weathered by the sun. Lisa had the body and mannerisms of a high school basketball player who controlled the inside lanes by sheer physical dominance. Lisa's kin had practically founded Leigh Acres without actually becoming the local gentry. You could say that Lisa lived on the wrong side of the tracks—even though both sides were now that side. Her husband, Earl, was a tall, lanky man, equally good-looking, with a slightly receding hairline that came with his forty-plus years. He looked like a plant foreman, but was the kind of guy that everyone knew and approached with a knowing grin like they shared some mischief as kids. Earl's family was likewise among the town's oldest inhabitants. In fact, their brick house was built overtop the cabin purchased by his grandfather years earlier. Earl had inherited the house upon Granddad's passing.

Hannah just turned forty-one. She was slightly shorter and more delicate with shiny black hair styled in a ponytail, with large, round glasses that frequently slipped down her nose. She would have looked like the girl next door had it not been for her striking dark eyes, petite frame, and olive skin. As she passed, middle-aged men were known to dreamily stare. Any random observer would guess her lineage to be anything from Mediterranean to Pacific Islander. But, she was the product of a Native American father and European mother and seemed to inherit the best of both worlds.

Early conversations between Hannah and Lisa disclosed that they had both been born within three months of each other, back in the 1970s. Each had a combination of good and bad experiences that formed them into who they were. Lisa had a previous husband and a combination of odd jobs, including short-order cook and a brief stint as a truck driver. She now had a good job coordinating shipments for a large manufacturing company.

Hannah, on the other hand, had finished college and landed a job with the Federal Bureau of Indian Affairs (BIA). A series of promotions led to becoming a project manager supervising residential home construction on tribal lands. After countless moves with new projects and a brief unsuccessful marriage, Hannah decided a change was in order and took a job at a small-town credit union in the Deep South. The town of Leigh Acres seemed to be the perfect place of refuge, or so she thought.

Hannah was briefly startled as Baxter the cat jumped onto her lap, depositing his overweight form. Hannah had sprung Baxter from "the joint," also known as the animal shelter, for company after long days on reservation construction sites. They were inseparable ever since, except for Lilly, another cat that joined the household courtesy of Earl. Lilly was small and demure with blue eyes and all white fur that hid a feisty temper developed from living on the streets. Baxter was a much larger calico, but deferred to Lilly because of his laid-back nature. He could typically be found lying under a shade tree watching a nearby squirrel, but not bothering to get up, lest he lose his comfortable spot.

Lisa, similarly, had sprung her beagle, Houdini, from a bad home down the block. Houdini was so named because he kept escaping from the neighbor's yard looking for a better situation, which he found at Lisa's.

"Looks like Baxter 'mixed it up' with another cat," observed Lisa, pointing to blood on Baxter's ear. Lisa tended to use phrases and a speaking style similar to men, given her various male-dominated occupations. But that actually worked well for Hannah, who had likewise survived in a male-dominated industry. Hannah checked Baxter over to make sure there wasn't more damage.

"I guess some other cat made insensitive comments about his weight," smiled Hannah, petting her friend. Baxter was almost fifteen and more than content to sit in Hannah's lap for an extended period, which he generally did. He would normally stay there until Lilly jumped up, indicating it was her turn.

The two sat for a few minutes longer until Lisa bid Hannah good night. "I have to check on Earl and do a PowerPoint for the boss before tomorrow," declared Lisa as she slowly got to her feet.

Lisa was well liked by the owner of the manufacturing plant who found that she had an unusual combination of skills that saved the plant buckets of money. She adeptly used softness and a southern accent to charm suppliers to meet impossible deadlines when needed. More importantly, she had a direct toughness that could clear red tape for truck drivers trying to deliver their load in record time. To top it all off, she had acquired some computer skills to do his PowerPoints.

"See you tomorrow," confirmed Hannah, rising with the cats scurrying behind.

Lisa paused her walk to turn around and say, "Speaking of spooky places, we can talk about what you and I have to do for the Fourth of July skirmish at the academy ruins." She then faded into the darkness that separated their two homes. Hannah had promised to help at the upcoming Civil War reenactment and fundraiser at the local historical site. But that was for another day, and time moved slowly here—lending itself to a good night's sleep—if she could keep her imagination in check.

Chapter 2
The Cotton Mill

Hannah awoke in the middle of the night and sat up with a start. The clock said 3:00 a.m. Baxter and Lilly took positions on the edge of the bed, observing Hannah's movements. Typically, Hannah would either be going to the restroom, which meant waiting to assume a warm spot on her return, or making a trip to the kitchen, where they always received a treat for following.

Hannah normally slept with the windows open, weather permitting, to enjoy the sounds of crickets and to catch a breeze rather than use the noisy air conditioner. Car headlights reflected off overgrown grass across the street as it drove to an area behind the abandoned cotton mill. The car disappeared into the grass, and then behind the building. Soon, a second car followed, and Hannah could hear the opening and closing of car doors. Moments later, two cars emerged from the grass as they made their way to the street. As they approached her house, Hannah ducked so they couldn't see her watching from her bedroom. This wasn't the first time this had happened. It seemed to occur sporadically at strange hours of the night.

Hannah lay in bed, scared and a little irritated. Nothing good happened at this time of night in a secluded area. Either drugs, prostitution, or some other big-city transaction had reached Leigh Acres. With both cars now gone, Hannah decided to put it out of her mind and try to get back to sleep. She drew some small consolation that Earl and Lisa were close by.

After work the next day, Hannah waded through the tall grass leading to the old mill to see what mischief had gone on the night before. On entering the building, her footsteps echoed on the old wooden floor. In the past, the sound was probably aesthetically pleasing, indicating people at work with gainful employment. Now, it was just hollow and creepy. The stillness of the mill illuminated by sporadic beams of light through broken windows created a feeling of foreboding. Hannah yelped as dripping water from the roof hit her shoulder, making her jump as if a specter of workers past touched her skin with icy hands. Hannah collected herself and moved from the large room to a side office, taking care not to slip on broken glass from a shattered window. The brick thrown by some troubled youth still lay as a testament to their crime of boredom.

Hannah then looked into each room, seeking the telltale signs of any vagrant, but found none. She did find a couple of spent hypodermic needles, which she carefully avoided. Hannah heard rustling outside as a man entered. She held her breath, thinking only of her vulnerability from having no weapon. She thought of the brick left on the floor but considered it too noisy to retreat back two rooms for its retrieval. The clearing of a man's throat was followed by, "Hannah, you in there?"

The recognition of Earl's voice brought immediate relief.

"Yeah, Earl," shouted Hannah, "I'm back here."

Hannah made her way back to the entrance as Earl met her in the center hallway. "What you doing in here? It's not safe," he mildly scolded.

"I'm sorry," responded Hannah, who went on to explain the midnight rendezvous by cars outside the building. She concluded with, "I was just seeing if there was something in here that was the object of their meeting."

"You should have called me," he admonished.

"Next time I'll do that," said Hannah apologetically. Then after a pause she asked, "So, what do you think they were up to?"

"Probably just drugs, I suppose," lamented Earl. "I've heard that there's a lot of drug and human trafficking on route to Memphis and Nashville."

Hannah had an instant look of fear. So, Earl quickly added, "But they're not from here—the traffickers, I mean. They just pass through the area. In fact, it's probably not traffickers way back here. The traffickers stay closer to the highway."

"So, what is going on here at night?" asked Hannah with genuine fear in her voice.

"Probably local users feeding their habit. They aren't interested in any of us. They're just normal people in the grips of addiction. Could be local businessmen and teachers for all we know." Earl seemed to have knowledge of just about anything involving human nature. It stood to reason that he would have equal insight into the seedier side of humanity.

"So, what can we do?" asked Hannah.

"I reckon that it's not the building itself that attracts them. It's the tall grass that camouflages their approach and whatever transaction they wish to hide," concluded Earl. He then put his arm in a sweeping motion toward Hannah's shoulder in a show of moving her out of the building without touching her. He was nothing if not a perfect gentleman. They moved out the back door to a small courtyard that led in two directions. "They meet and drive off in opposite directions as if nothing happened. One car goes downtown and the other goes out to the country."

In truth, downtown and the country were only a couple blocks apart, but the logic was sound.

"So. If it's the tall grass that attracts them, would the city cut the grass if I asked?" inquired Hannah, almost pleading.

"No," said Earl, shaking his head. "I could call a buddy working at the town hall, but I already know the answer. A couple years back, the city did just that and sent a bill for their services to Old Man Warner, who owns the mill. He fired it right back and told them to stay off his property."

Hannah understood. The whole town seemed to be owned by families that had moved into nicer digs in the nearby countryside or the big city. After they extracted their fortunes from the town, there was no reason to stay.

"No. Here in the South, the rule is, If'n you don't like the view, you either have to buy it or fix it yourself," said Earl with an exaggerated drawl to reinforce the authenticity of the quote.

After a pause, Hannah concluded, "So, I have to cut the lawn myself."

"Wait a minute," objected Earl. "If anybody's going to cut it, I am."

"No, you're not. I'm perfectly capable of cutting it with a riding lawn mower," said Hannah with confidence. In reality, she had never driven one before, but she wasn't about to have Earl take this on because of her fear.

After debating the point back and forth for a minute, Earl finally gave in. "I have a riding mower you can use and we can take turns."

Hannah paused and reviewed the large grassy area. It approached about an acre all around.

"No," she concluded. "That's too much for your mower given that your yard is over an acre already. I've been meaning to get a riding mower anyway to take care of the abandoned lots on either side of me. I just have to find something affordable."

Earl grudgingly nodded in agreement. They both knew that Hannah lived to work outside, or rejoiced in trying some remodel project after doing credit union business all day. Earl, on the other hand, came home to collapse after a hard day in the sun. Plus, Earl already cut his own yard and Hannah's too over her objections.

"I know a guy we can get a mower from," said Earl after some brief thought.

Hannah just chuckled. The world may be filled with uncertainty but there was one thing that was never in doubt. Earl always knew a guy that owed him a favor. In this particular case, it would be a guy with a line on a riding mower.

The next afternoon, Hannah took delivery of an old lawn mower.

"So, this is it," said Lisa, approaching.

"This is it," said Hannah, looking pleased at her slightly used, or greatly used, John Deere tractor astride a lawn-cutting platform. Its classic green chassis stood out against newly shined yellow-rimmed tires.

"Should we wait for Earl for a driving lesson?" asked Lisa.

"No, I can handle this. I've watched my father do it a hundred times."

Hannah climbed aboard and worked through what her father usually did and thought out loud as she went. "Pull out the throttle—check. Push the clutch and move gear lever to neutral—check. Press the brake—check. Turn the key—check." The engine protested, then sprang to life. After putting it in gear, she lurched forward. After an hour of serious grass cutting, Hannah retired the mower and sprayed water from a cold hose in her face. Lisa had been watching and walked over.

They moved to the front porch, where Lisa handed her an iced tea she'd retrieved from Hannah's kitchen.

Then their eyes were drawn simultaneously to the graffiti exposed on the lower walls of the cotton mill previously obscured by the tall grass. It included a couple cryptic icons that seemed to be gang symbols.

"It almost looked better with the grass."

"We'll just get some gray paint to match the cotton mill and paint over it," announced Lisa.

"Are we inviting some retribution from a gang if we cover up their symbols?" asked Hannah with slight fear in her voice.

"It's been years. Whoever did it isn't even around anymore."

"Okay. I hate the way it looks. If I'm going to do this, I might as well be all in. That's the only way to dissuade midnight callers *and* make it look nice for the neighborhood."

"I agree. I'll have Earl bring home some rollers left over from a job site. We'll do it tomorrow." Luckily, Earl worked for his brother-in-law, who refurbished old buildings and converted them to lofts and office spaces. He knew how to do just about anything. And, if he couldn't do it himself, he knew somebody who could— and they owed him a favor.

The following day, Hannah bought some paint and retrieved a couple of roller pans left from her own home improvement efforts. Hannah and Lisa started on the graffiti only to be joined by two of Earl's friends. They were among several friends who helped to tend Earl and Lisa's community garden. It was well known in the neighborhood that anybody needing food should help themselves. More than one family took advantage of the plot that had become a mainstay of the little town.

In less than thirty minutes, the job was done and everyone retreated to Lisa's driveway for a beverage. Hopefully, the midnight callers would stop.

Chapter 3
The Skirmish

Two days later on Independence Day, Hannah sat on the porch drinking her morning iced tea while enjoying the view of the cotton mill's freshly cut grass and graffitiless siding. It was already turning hot, which wasn't unexpected in the Deep South. The sun had just peeked over the adjacent cotton mill, illuminating sporadic broken windows behind the tall grass. Lisa approached in her Hyundai Sonata and rolled down the window.

"Are you off?" asked Hannah, now standing.

"Yes, I promised Earl's father that I'd be there by eight to help with the food. Earl's already been there for two hours setting up," said Lisa with a yawn.

"Okay, I'll be there right behind you at nine," said Hannah as she walked back to the porch. Lisa waved a final goodbye as she rounded the corner onto the town's main street, two blocks long.

Today was the annual Civil War Skirmish at LaGrange Military Academy, or what was now the anthropological remnants of LaGrange Military Academy. The historical marker at the site identified the former school as "The West Point of the South." The school was long gone, but the site remained along with a few Civil War-era buildings including a small store, post office, log cabin, barn, church, one-room museum, and pavilion. A cemetery sat adjacent to the site on a hill not visible to most visitors. If you ever find occasion to visit this park, it's best to refer to the

Civil War as the "War Between the States," or better yet, "War of Northern Aggression." Most people don't care one way or the other, but a few supporters of the cause might still take offense.

Hannah had promised Lisa to assist in cooking burgers at the annual Fourth of July fundraiser and Civil War Skirmish. It had originally been a reenactment of a Civil War battle but had dwindled to just a little dust-up known in reenactment circles as a skirmish.

Hannah showered and dressed in a pair of shorts and a tank top with a loose cotton blouse overtop to manage working in the summer heat. She made the four-mile drive expecting to park near the hilltop site. As she approached the foothill leading to the park's entrance, an elderly flagman in an orange vest had other ideas. Hannah looked on as he frantically waved his red flag toward a makeshift parking lot in an adjacent field. Hannah groaned and waved back her compliance. The festivities didn't start for another three hours, and Hannah had hoped to avoid the quarter-mile hike up the winding mountain road by parking in one of the limited open areas by the site. As the solitary car, her consolation prize was having plenty of places to choose from. After selecting a spot under a tree, Hannah hauled three folding chairs out of the back of her little white pickup for herself, Earl, and Lisa.

"Got to manage your husband's truck, I see," he observed with a smirk.

"Actually, it's mine," replied Hannah with a smile. She used it to carry a small ladder and tools, which she used on her bank inspections of homes under construction to verify the completion of critical phases of electrical, plumbing, and other milestones, before releasing funds. She thought about explaining her utilitarian need of a truck but decided to let it go. She would just leave him to wonder if she was one of those "women's libbers" who insisted on driving a pickup.

"You're starting early—parking the cars, I mean," commented Hannah, trying not to sound irritated as she now stood in front of the old man's self-created guard post.

"Yep, got to save spots on the hilltop for dignitaries."

"When does the shuttle start?" she asked hopefully. She was told that ROTC students from the state college in the nearby town normally shuttled visitors in long golf carts up the hill to the entrance, where awaiting elderly ladies sold entry tickets from an old tin box.

"Ain't come yet. Not for another two hours," said the old man unapologetically.

Hannah wanted to say, *Two hours? Are you crazy? So we have to crawl up this hill in July heat to save a parking spot for your buddy, the grand poohbah of the loyal order of water buffaloes?* But she didn't.

She just smiled and said, "Then I guess I'll just have to walk," and started up the hill.

After a quarter mile up the winding slope, Hannah took a moment's break to survey the scene from the white fence marking the site's entrance. At least the old ticket takers weren't there yet. Lisa warned Hannah that they normally extracted the $10 entrance fee even from protesting volunteers, reasoning that every little bit counted.

Hannah walked through the entrance another fifty yards, through a central grass rotunda of sorts, to deposit the chairs next to the old grill. It was loosely called a grill, being more in appearance like an oil drum with the top half opening on hinges. Lisa's husband had dragged the old monster out of a nearby shed and cleaned it up at the crack of dawn. Earl and Lisa had married just five years earlier, but still had that "new marrieds" relationship and greatly enjoyed each other's company. Earl had likewise taken a maternal interest in Hannah's well-being and was protective of her safety. Hannah liked knowing that Earl and Lisa were just a shout or phone call away if trouble arose.

Hannah and Lisa would be working over this grill in two hours. Their spot was ideal given its proximity between the old pavilion, which sold the traditional local favorite, chicken stew, and an old state fair food trailer selling the burgers and hot dogs prepared by Hannah and Lisa. Lisa had also warned Hannah to bring her own buns because the folks in the concession trailer were in league with the ticket sellers and would extract the price of food from all volunteers, including the cooks, Hannah and Lisa. Hannah brought three buns for herself, Lisa, and Earl to sneak their lunch hot off the grill and out of site of the food police. Besides, she needed to keep up her strength after the grueling climb up the mountain.

Hannah glanced around the site looking for Lisa and saw a couple small tents preparing to sell everything from fudge to jewelry. None of the vendors today would sell anything even remotely associated with the Civil War, or the school, but they had to have something to justify the $10 admission without a full battle as in years past. Hannah turned to look at the field adjacent to the site to estimate how many Civil War reenactors were present. She counted just two pup tents. Hannah calculated that each probably housed two of what she was told were "hardcore" reenactors. The other, less zealous reenactors, called FARBS ("far be it from authentic"), slept at home and would arrive shortly.

Earl had explained that diehard reenactment participants came in different forms. Some were known to go on crash diets for weeks or months before the reenactment season to look like skinny, half-starved Southern soldiers just like in the Civil War. When they did eat, they were said to reject good apples in favor of battered and bruised versions typical of those consumed by foraging soldiers. Based on Hannah's estimation, there would be a total of eight reenactors for the skirmish, barely enough to drag out the spectacle for the crowd for half an hour. Even the loudly grieving widows in period gowns rushing to their expiring men couldn't extent the show that much. Just then, Lisa walked up and gave her a hug.

Reading Hannah's mind, Lisa said, "I hear they got two men with horses to play the cavalry coming and two more to shoot the cannon. I hope that will be enough to make it worth the $10 admission."

"They'll put on a good show," affirmed Hannah with a smile. Hannah knew this event was important to Earl because it was important to Earl's father—the main volunteer. And, if it was important to Earl, Lisa was going to do everything in her power to make it a success—even if that meant coercing some truck drivers that owed her a favor to fill volunteer spots.

Earl walked up already covered in sweat. Lisa grabbed his hand and led him to a chair. Hannah spotted some bottled water in ice and retrieved it.

"That woman's going to drive me nuts," said Earl.

"What woman?" said Lisa, looking around, ready to take her on.

"Henrietta, the wife of Elmer at the bottom of the hill. She's as wacky as he is. She had me drag out some old junk from one of the barns to sell on a table. It's some household stuff from the '70s that has nothing to do with the school or the Civil War. But, she's convinced somebody will buy it. Look, I saved one of the items for you to look at," he said, exasperated, as he handed Lisa a Barbie doll with the head missing.

Lisa smiled and handed it to Hannah. "Any interest? I'm sure it's a steal."

Hannah smiled. "Even though I recognize it as the elusive 'Malibu Barbie,' I guess I'd still prefer the head."

Hannah then turned to Earl. "You get right back in there and find the head," she said sternly, shaking her finger in his face like an old school marm.

They all had a laugh as they sat in the lawn chairs. Then, Henrietta could be seen fast approaching in a golf cart. She was all of eighty-five with badly dyed jet black hair that looked like the style Priscilla Presley wore when she met Elvis. She was looking rapidly from side to side when Hannah realized Earl was probably the object of her search. He noticed too and got a terrified look. Then, he scurried behind the pavilion.

Henrietta sped up on her golf cart. "Lisa, have you seen Earl? I could have sworn he was just here."

"Earl? My Earl? No, I haven't. Have you seen him, Hannah?" asked Lisa as she looked around.

"I don't think so," Hannah said, trying to drive home the illusion by looking around in confusion. She then stood in front of the recently vacated chair to hide the headless Malibu Barbie laying in a contorted position like roadkill.

"Well, if you see Earl, tell him I have a very important job for him," she said as she pressed on the accelerator, barely missing another volunteer.

After a minute, Lisa said in the direction of the pavilion, "You can come out now, Earl—she's gone."

Earl came back relieved and sat. "She is such a dingbat."

There was a rumor that the reason there were so few reenactors each year was because they were tired of Henrietta ordering them around as their self-appointed commander-in-chief. It was also normally understood that reenactors would be fed before and after any event. Henrietta departed from the longstanding tradition and extracted the price of food from them, just like the volunteers.

"Tell me more about LaGrange," said Hannah, watching some newly arrived local vendors arranging a few trinkets for sale to visitors on their folding tables.

"Well," said Earl, fishing out a badly needed cigarette from his blue T-shirt pocket. Even a nonsmoker would take up the habit after an hour working with Henrietta. "The military academy was started by the local preacher before the war on the school grounds vacated by another college that moved to Florence. I heard it was just a few cadets but grew quickly because there weren't no other colleges back then, till Alabama came along," said Earl with veiled disgust. He was referring to the University of Alabama, about three hours away in the middle of the state. Earl, like most people in North Alabama, was an Auburn fan. Lisa, on the other hand, was a diehard Alabama fan, their rival. It was said that Auburn drew more students from the country with its agricultural programs and conservative values. Conversely, the University of Alabama recruited more from the big cities like Birmingham. Hannah could feel his pain. She graduated from Marquette in Wisconsin, which had a similar basketball rivalry with the larger University of Wisconsin.

"The military academy only accepted boys, like most colleges of the time," continued Earl. "The school grew until the War Between the States, when most cadets were conscripted by the Confederacy."

"So the academy replaced the original college that moved and became the University of North Alabama?" asked Hannah.

"Yep," confirmed Earl. The University of North Alabama had grown to a respectable size, drawing from local towns in Alabama, Tennessee, and Mississippi, where it sat in the state's northwest corner astride the three states.

After sitting for a moment, Lisa declared, "We better get going and start preparing the food before the 'dingbat' rats us out."

With that, they all rose. Earl put wood into the old grill to get it heated up for the burgers and hot dogs that would supply the food trailer. The grill handle was broken a few years prior and now had a crescent wrench, jury-rigged by Earl, to raise and lower the lid.

To Hannah's surprise, a decent crowd arrived in time for lunch. As a result, Hannah and Lisa were kept busy cooking and shuttling burgers and dogs to the nearby concession trailer in large baking tins. As quickly as the crowd came, they departed to set up their lawn chairs bordering the field that would serve as the battlefront for the reenactment.

Two cannoneers lit the first fuse, creating an ear-splitting boom to start the scrimmage. Earl had returned just in time to tap Hannah on the shoulder. He handed her toilet paper, saying only, "Stuff it in your ears." Hannah inserted a wad of paper in each ear while some bystanders with crying kids retreated for the rear. On cue, eight "rebs" emerged from the tall grass on one side of the field and charged to meet three "Yankees" from the other.

"They might win this time," commented Hannah, who saw the grievously outnumbered Yankees.

"Those reenactors," observed Earl, "are local boys who hold a drawing to see who has to wear the three Yankee uniforms. The losers ain't too happy to be wearing the Union blue. The winners get to wear Confederate gray."

As they watched, the two "armies" stopped about thirty yards apart, kneeled, and shot. After the first volley, two Confederates fell dying.

"How do they make sure they don't all die at once? They have to make this last at least thirty minutes," asked Hannah.

"They have a drawing for that too. Nobody wants to die in the first volleys because they have to lie in the grass too long. That is, unless they're tasked to be wounded and dying, then they're dragged to the medical tent."

Almost as if hearing Earl, two wailing women in period gowns ran to the dying men, pulling them to their breasts for a brief cry before helping them limp to the hospital tent.

"How many fatalities do we expect?" asked a grinning Hannah.

Earl turned to her and said, "Don't laugh. Some of them reenactors can be ornery. They've been known to put staples in their homemade blanks to make it sting if they shoot close enough. A couple years back, they had to take a guy to the hospital that got cut badly by the staple-filled ball at close range."

"Really?" remarked an incredulous Hannah.

"Yep. Now they actually inspect the shot before the skirmish to make sure there ain't no shenanigans," affirmed Earl.

After a couple more volleys that took almost five minutes to casually load (presumably much longer than a real soldier shooting for his life), the two-horse cavalry arrived and ran off the remaining pair of Yankees. With a final shot of the cannon, the skirmish was over. Sporadic clapping followed from the thin crowd.

"So, that's it?" asked Hannah.

"That's it," confirmed Lisa. The little crowd gathered their chairs and blankets to make their slow march down the hill to their cars. Earl got up and left to start some park-closing chores.

"How many more years can they do this?" asked Hannah.

"I don't know. Maybe one or two. No more than that," said Lisa.

"It's a shame," said Hannah.

"Yes," lamented Lisa. "I worry about Earl. He's devoted to his father and doesn't know what EJ will do with hisself when they don't do this anymore. It's the park's big moneymaker for the year. And they need that money to keep going."

Earl's father, now eighty-five, spent a few hours each day at the LaGrange Military Academy site with little fix-it jobs and landscaping.

"So, Earl's afraid that if EJ doesn't have this, he'll wither away?" asked Hannah with a frown.

"Well, speak of the devil," said Lisa, almost as a warning to stop talking in the spirit of good manners. Hannah looked on as Earl's father, EJ, approached on a golf cart. EJ was slim like his son Earl with an age-spotted bald head and slightly hunched body. He drove the golf cart with his hands clutching the wheel at the ten and two o'clock positions reserved for those with a learner's permit or glaucoma. "How'd you manage to get the cart away from you-know-who?"

EJ looked up at the sky, exasperated, but said only, "Bless her heart."

Hannah had learned it was customary in the South to utter this statement typically before or after an unkind work or gossip about an individual. That way, it didn't make it seem unkind.

"Actually, I came to see Hannah," said EJ, grunting as he pulled himself off the golf cart. Hannah pulled a chair over to the aging man, who gladly accepted it.

"What can I do for you, EJ?" asked Hannah.

"It's what I can do for you, young lady. I hear you're a history buff."

"Yes," confirmed Hannah, "guilty as charged."

"Well, I wanted to offer up the old school journals for your reading."

"Really? What kind of journals?" asked Hannah with unusual excitement.

"Just various books from the Military Academy including old supply ledgers, a sick log, and such. We keep it all in the vault at the library," said EJ, wiping his forehead in the July heat. Lisa went to fetch him an iced tea to keep him hydrated.

"They must be valuable to be kept in the vault. Are you sure you want to lend them out?" asked Hannah.

The approaching Lisa laughed. "The vault is just the holdover from the old bank that became converted to the library. It's really just a closet."

"I'd love to read the journals," said Hannah, "and vault-worthy or not, I'll be sure to take good care of them."

"Great. I'll tell Bert the librarian that you may be stopping by," said EJ, now rising. A worried look on his face indicated that the "dingbat" was rapidly approaching the little group to take back her golf cart.

All three arose and tried to look busy and innocent of any crime lest they be pulled into some job. Successful, they slipped away with the crowd and retreated home.

Chapter 4
The Vault

Hannah ducked out of work early to reach the library as it opened at 2:30 p.m. The local high school got out at 3:00, so the Leigh Acres library opened just before and long enough to prepare the four old PCs used by students for projects. On seeing her, Bert unlocked the library and flicked on the lights, with Hannah following quickly behind.

Dust seemed everywhere the eye could see. There were even spider webs woven around some books. However, the old mahogany shelves still found a way to present their stately presence through the grime. Dust floated lazily, causing Hannah to involuntarily stop her breathing as a reflex due to her allergies. The books themselves seemed well kept and neatly organized with the spines facing outward and arranged by genre, including westerns, mysteries, children's books, and so on. The left wall contained folding tables with the student computers and a section of old VHS tapes, long replaced by live streaming for visual entertainment. The far-right wall contained a glass case displaying some old Indian artifacts.

Hannah had been told that Bert wasn't really a librarian, but a retired factory foreman. He looked the part of the factory foreman with a large frame and a beard in need of a trim. It being a voluntary position, Bert met the primary qualification—free time, with an emphasis on *free*.

"So, you're the librarian?" commented Hannah, making conversation.

"Yes, my wife, Muriel, and I take turns," he said, going behind the checkout desk; literally a small school desk by the front door. "I hear from EJ you have an interest in history. Would you like to see our Native American artifacts before we get to the records and books?"

"Sure," said Hannah. "Do you know what tribes they're from?"

Bert looked at her as if thinking, *Why would that matter?* He obviously didn't know about Hannah's stint working for the Bureau of Indian Affairs. She had visited tribes ranging from the Inuit in Alaska to the Navaho in New Mexico.

"Some Choctaw, Creek, and other tribes," he responded. "They stopped to rest here on their way to Oklahoma during the Trail of Tears."

"Really," commented a surprised Hannah, pausing to push up her glasses after bending over the case. "They stopped at Leigh Acres on their way west?"

"Some already lived in Alabama, but most came from other southern states. The townspeople took pity on them and gave them food. Some returned gifts for their hospitality. Do you know anything about the Trail of Tears?" asked Bert, sensing that Hannah knew more about the subject than most.

"I believe that ten years before the Civil War, there was a government-assisted land grab to seize the tribe members' farms to expand cotton plantations. Over a hundred thousand Native Americans were forced to walk the thousand-plus miles to Oklahoma. In addition to losing their land and livestock, many lost their lives."

"That's right," exclaimed Bert. "Those poor wretches passed through these parts and received some kindness from the local impoverished farmers who empathized with their plight. How is it that you know so much?"

"My father was a member of Lac du Flambeau tribe of Chippewa Indians from around Lake Superior," answered Hannah politely, but she stopped there. She found that most people she encountered treated her differently, often with some suspicion, after learning she was Native American with intimate knowledge of her lineage. It was as if they expected her to show up with a sign protesting something. But, Bert was different.

"I've heard of the Chippewa because of my interest in the artifacts. They are the largest tribe in North America around the Great Lakes, not just Lake Superior, right?" asked Bert excitedly because he found somebody with potentially the same interests.

"That's right. The Chippewa nation covers several Midwest states. They also cover part of Canada with over 150 different individual tribes. We tend to call them communities now, instead of tribes. My particular community acquired the name from French trappers that watched them gather fish by torchlight. The name means 'Lake of the Torches' in French. In fact, my mother was a descendent from French trappers who settled in the area."

"So, that's why I didn't take you for Native American. But now that you say that, I can see the features," said Bert with transparent sincerity.

"You're right. People can't quite place me," said Hannah. "As a little girl, I felt a little self-conscious, but now I think it makes me unique."

"That's a good thing," concurred Bert.

Hannah politely looked over the glass case and asked a few questions about the various pieces. Then, after a prolonged silence as if in memoriam for the people who died, Bert asked, "So, do you know EJ well?"

"Not really well. I recently started working at the credit union and moved into the old cotton mill overseer house next to EJ's son Earl and his wife. We became friends and I volunteered to help them at the July 4th reenactment. EJ picked up that I'm a history buff with an interest in the LaGrange Military Academy." Hannah's house was only fifty yards from the library's back door across an empty lot so Bert knew exactly where she lived.

"I heard that old Mrs. O'Reilly sold the place. You're sprucing it up?"

Hannah had painted the little cottage and fixed the old shed just behind. She also repaired and painted the old shutters black around all the windows, making it match some of the classic southern homes in the area.

"Yes," confirmed Hannah, "but I need another hobby and like researching history. In fact, I brought a couple books I'd like to donate to the library if you want them."

"That's fine," agreed Bert. "We don't get many new books in good condition. I'll read them to make sure they're all right and then put them on the shelf. Let me show you where we keep the old academy journals. There's mainly just old ledgers and military logs recording comings and goings by the cadets on watch and such. I'll just need your driver's license to get you a library card. We can make a note regarding what you take."

"That's great," said Hannah, withdrawing her license from her designer purse. That was Hannah's one vice. She liked expensive purses. She handed over the license and gazed across at the boxes of books in the small storeroom with a bank-like vault door. "I'm surprised to see a door like this. Any of the contents valuable?"

"Not so much," lamented Bert, "this was the bank's former main office years back. It closed after a fire and moved up the street." Hannah worked for a competitor of theirs and was totally ignorant of its past. She just knew it as a place she competed with to fund local building projects. "The bank donated the building decades ago, including the vault door," concluded Bert.

Hannah looked uncomfortably at the door as she entered the little space. "Do you have the key?"

"No, but don't worry. It hasn't been closed in years."

Hannah watched the retreating old man with some trepidation. Every horror movie she'd ever seen came flooding back with the victim locked safely away, never to be heard from again. Shaking it off, she entered the room and started digging through a box of academy material. Hopefully, she'd live to see another day.

Chapter 5
The Journal

After leaving the library, Hannah went into her meager pantry and made a dinner of Spam Lite and Cheetos. *We'll find out if the "lite" version has the same culinary quality of regular Spam,* thought Hannah. Unlike people who ate junk food on the go, Hannah just liked it. She would pick a cheeseburger and Cheetos over steak and a baked potato every time.

After what was loosely called dinner, Hannah decided that Spam Lite was, in fact, remarkably similar to regular Spam. Her conclusion was that their similarity might be good or bad, depending on a person's culinary palette. She then decided that some exercise was in order and made her way to Lisa's. Weight control never seemed to be a problem for Hannah despite a horrific diet of junk food, much to the consternation of friends. But it was a warm summer evening typical for the rural South, so she felt less guilty about her eating habits given that anybody would burn the calories despite their metabolism with activity in this heat.

She met Lisa and Earl in their usual spot, relaxing in lawn chairs on their driveway in front of a large fan. The fan was actually a discarded industrial attic fan that Earl had retrieved from an old building he was renovating. He loosely covered the face with chicken wire so somebody accidently reaching within wouldn't lose a finger, or worse. Even covered, it looked nasty and sounded like an old car engine, but it could cool half a neighborhood and certainly earned its keep.

A lazy conversation ensued about the local police cruiser that seemed to be doing a robust ticket business tonight.

"Got another one," commented Lisa.

"That's probably three in the last half hour," confirmed Hannah.

The local police typically sat in a small alley between the old dry goods store and the cotton mill, hidden from view by motorists approaching the old railroad tracks. People hurrying home from work often failed to come to a complete stop at the traffic signs straddling the tracks. Locals knew not only to stop completely but wait a few seconds before proceeding. Protestations to the contrary were ignored and warnings were unheard of.

"I guess somebody has to pay to power the street lights," said Lisa with a sigh. Leigh Acres had nothing in the way of revenue. The downtown was boarded up and there would certainly be no new businesses anytime soon with the possible exception of Dollar General. A rumor was circulating that their Town Creek location, frequented by Leigh Acres residents after driving fifteen miles, was exceedingly profitable. So, the scuttlebutt was that Dollar General was considering expansion into Leigh Acres. At least, that's what people said. But that wasn't the first rumor of some new business or outside investment. The year before, people swore that a country western music theme park was being planned that would rival Disney World. Hannah contemplated the outcome if both actually came into being. It would probably lead to alleged sightings of Elvis at the Dollar General. They sat for a couple more minutes watching the police officer deliver yet another ticket and resumed their conversation.

"Did Bert retrieve the old academy records for you?" asked Lisa.

"Yes," confirmed Hannah. "He sent me into the old vault to take what I needed."

"So, you went into the old vault?" challenged Earl. He seemed to have a natural protectiveness of both women.

"Creepy, isn't it?" added Lisa.

"Yep. I didn't see any chainsaws, so I took a chance and went in," countered Hannah as if to say *don't worry about me.*

"Did you find anything good?" asked Lisa.

Hannah described the box but hadn't really looked at the books and papers, so their contents were still anybody's guess.

"I was thinking I'd start reading them tonight," said Hannah guiltily as she enjoyed the lazy day of summer. Lisa just nodded in agreement as they sat watching the police car move back to its hiding place in the alley.

"It was sure nice of EJ to get me access," continued Hannah. It was clear she was stalling any academic endeavor for the evening. But Hannah knew EJ had taken it upon himself to share his interest in the old military academy and she was intent on making an effort. Finally, with the conversation waning, she couldn't put off going home any longer and bid Lisa and Earl good night.

She arrived at home and gave the cats their treats. Treats always accompanied any entry into the house. Hannah moved to the couch with the musty old box on the living room table. She removed the books that appeared to be reasonably held in place with cracked and worn bindings. She then neatly arranged them on the coffee table by type. Some were standard ledgers associated with the military, which made sense given that the school was an academy. Among these books were two watch logs, a sick call log, a mail log, and a quartermaster's log indicating an inventory of supplies received and payments made. She then retrieved a few loose papers including a deed and land survey of the school.

Finally, under some loose papers she found a peculiar leather pouch with a wax seal large enough to contain a book. The seal itself made her pause, wondering if it was intended to be confidential. Then she reasoned that after 150 years, nothing could really be considered secret or a personal invasion of privacy. So, she opened the leather pouch to find a personal journal of a cadet, Caleb Rochester. There was no note as to why it was retained or why somebody had sealed it. Hannah opened the journal and began reading. She quickly found that it was a cross between a cadet's notes and personal observations. Hannah began slowly reading its first entry in handwritten script and unfamiliar language from a bygone era.

*****

August 4, 1860

I finished my first week at LaGrange Military Academy. Being from a dirt farm, I find that I'm different than most of the other boys that hail from plantations. I came to be here after my father; a sullen man, sat me down and provided counsel against what he saw as my propensity for dreaming. He observed that I spent excessive time reading tales of any kind from Ivanhoe to Shakespeare. I also had an inclination for being found near my grandfather whom I begged to expostulate on his service in the Continental Army. But after much contemplation, my father decided that I might be well introduced to middle society and raise my fortunes, by industry in a school of higher learning associated with my interest in adventure and the military. Furthermore, he expounded that a school with a military course of study should provide conditions by which I would neither to aspire for wealth by risk, nor poverty by in-application. The school would place me on the road to the middle station of society, which he found through long experience, to be the most suited to happiness without excessive sufferings—except that by which our Lord and Savior allows for the betterment of our character. The military aspect of my education would further remove any distempers and weakness of body. It would also teach me by way of discipline to avoid envy and a lust of ambition. On the matter of war, he pressed me earnestly to attain an officer's rank and the skills of administration. In the case of conflict, that would allow me to avoid hardship or death. In the case of peace, I might be introduced to the mercantile exchange from which to gain civilian employment.

He further observed that I, in most ways, take after my fair and petite mother, in contrast to himself with a more robust and stout stature lending itself to his being a farmer. That life, he explained, exposed a man to much hardship from labor in addition to potential disaster from flood, drought and other general calamity. In my more gentle physical state, the potential for excessive labor was that much again greater. No, he exclaimed, enrollment in a military academy of higher learning was for me. As a result, I find myself, after a week, far from home in a strange place requiring much adjustment of thought and temperament.

*****

Hannah looked at the clock and was surprised to see that it was after midnight. It had taken over two hours to decipher the almost illegible writing to extract Caleb's thoughts. Besides, her cats were watching quizzically, like, *What are you still doing up?* She took the hint and gave them their pre-bed treat, not to be confused with their late-evening, post-dinner treat.

Hannah retired to her bedroom only to see the headlight of a car stop short of the newly cut grass surrounding the cotton mill. Hannah automatically moved away from the window lest she be seen as nosy. After slight hesitation, the car continued down the street and rounded the corner rather than proceed to what she assumed would be a rendezvous with a drug dealer. She was happy that it worked but tried to shake off the feeling of foreboding and retired to a fitful sleep.

Chapter 6
Cadet Life

After returning from work the next day, Hannah stopped at a gas station to buy dinner. It wasn't like most, but more like a combination of a full-service garage with three repair bays from yesteryear and a modern convenience store with more items than typically carried. It made sense given the lack of fast food and grocers nearby. Tonight, she was in the mood for pizza (heated under a lamp and sold by the slice) and a candy bar for dessert. This was Hannah's typical menu. Sometimes she would splurge and get two gas station hot dogs cooked by a light bulb. Once she asked the counter help if she could get hers medium-well lit. They didn't see the humor.

Hannah approached the man behind the counter. He seemed fairly well dressed in an oxford button-down shirt and khaki pants. In contrast to typical counter help who absentmindedly worked to fill orders in an old T-shirt and jeans, he moved with confidence and attention to detail as if he owned the place, which she assumed he did.

Following her divorce, Hannah decided that her books and two cats were more reliable companions than any man. And probably more interesting too. But she had her moments.

This particular man wasn't wearing a ring and looked like her archetype of the perfect mate. He was medium build with little streaks of gray in his hair and projected a quiet confidence, like herself. So, Hannah decided to venture out if just for a moment.

"How are you today?" she asked.

"Fine," he said.

After an awkward silence where Hannah couldn't think of any item of conversation, she finally said, "I was hoping to buy pizza."

"What kind, pepperoni or cheese? They're both good if I do say so myself. The slices are pretty big. One or two can serve as a meal," he said while walking toward the heat lamp case.

"Two pepperoni," answered Hannah. She then became self-conscious about the quantity and had the urge to explain that she didn't gain weight easily, but let it pass. Two customers simultaneously entered with the no-patience look of needing to buy cigarettes.

"Anything else?" he said while cheerily ringing up the purchase.

"Just these GooGoos," she said, feeling even more self-conscious. GooGoos were a candy bar favorite of the region—normally purchased by school kids with very permissive parents.

Hannah took her food and left thinking *that could have gone better*. Since this place met the qualifications to become her favorite culinary spot, she would have another try. Maybe next week, if she didn't have a heart attack from this dinner first.

Hannah sat on the front porch enjoying pizza and her Original GooGoo. She considered choosing the Supreme but thought she'd wait for a special occasion. The only other choice was peanut butter flavored, which she wasn't partial to. She munched on her treat while watching a blue bird at her bird feeder. Hannah was a self-acknowledged animal freak who fed just about anything. She recently began leaving food for a possum living under her garden shed, hoping that possum wasn't the natural enemy of cats. If there was an altercation, the possum would just play dead, right?

Animals served an important role in the beliefs of her father's tribe. Tribal lore stated that all animals had souls or spirits, just like people. In fact, some animals served as spirit guides that would teach and guide a person through life—sometimes even protecting them. While Hannah became an evangelical Christian with a different view, she still retained the love and respect for animals. This translated into a large grocery bill for everything from bird seed to cat food. Luckily, cat food served double duty for possums in need.

After her dinner, Hannah returned to the journal and found that she was learning to read Caleb's thoughts with slightly greater ease and speed. It started to come together as if watching a movie in her mind. A scene unfolded with Caleb trying to adjust to the pitfalls of academy life.

*****

Three senior cadets approached Caleb at his bunk.

"So, they're taking in street urchins from bug holes now," said the largest boy, whom Caleb knew by the name Bull. He seemed every bit his namesake with a flat nose, a neck that seemed to span the width of his shoulders. and black eyes. He towered a head taller than his two lackeys, who seemed to enjoy playing any part in intimidating his victims.

"I ain't no street urchin. I come from my father's farm," objected Caleb.

"Makes no difference. Just some tenant farmer who got throwed out of the north. They is all just the same in them northern counties," jeered Bull.

"Ain't neither," objected Caleb, now standing face to face with the bully. Or, more accurately, face to chest. "My grandpap got the homestead in a land grant fair and square after he fought in the revolution. It's more than your 'flicker' (cowardly) kin can say."

With that provocation, Bull pushed Caleb and caused him to fall backwards over his steamer trunk contained at the foot of his bunk. Caleb tried to right himself as the other two boys circled behind. They were about to hold him when a third cadet entered the room. He saw what was happening and pushed his way between Caleb and the two. "You harassed the fresh fish long enough. If you boys don't move on, I'll 'sockdologer' (punch) you so hard you'll be swimmy-headed for a week."

Caleb's savior's ruddy appearance made him "a sight of some natural fear." Or, they knew him from some similar incident that ended with their ears being boxed. Either way, they immediately withdrew behind their large companion. Caleb's rescuer then addressed the large boy and said, "Move along now. I won't be askin' twice."

Silence ensued while the Bull contemplated his odds, which were good but not worth the licks he'd take himself. Then he turned to his companions and said, "Leave these two iron-clad possum eaters to themselves. When we're 'brass hats' (officers), they'll both be taking orders from us anyway."

Caleb and his new friend stood silently until the danger was gone.

After they left, the boy turned and thrust his hand forward. "The name's Ridge. Don't let them boys raise your temper. They just heard there was another lad from Winston County."

"You're from Winston County?" asked Caleb.

"Yep. I hail from around Black Creek."

"Our farm ain't far from there over the holler. My name's Caleb. Why do they dislike us so?"

Ridge pointed to two steamer trunks and they sat opposite each other as he explained, "Two of them sound-on-the-goose boys hail from Montgomery, and the other codfish aristocrat comes from Jefferson County down Birmingham way. Them areas to the south have large plantations that use slaves to perform all the plowing and such that you and I do with a mule. They see us as working class that should consider them as our betters."

"I don't see that living off the sweat of other men makes you any better. Every man should earn his own way," said Caleb.

"You and I see eye to eye. Don't worry. I figger they'll be leavin' you alone from now on. Like you said, they're nothing but flickers anyway."

The two sat a while longer and caught up on news from home. They both seemed to feel a sense of loss as shared memories were replaced by the cold sterility of barracks life and boys who seemed to attack any perceived weakness. The only joys found now would be the temporary absence of fear.

"I'll ask the cadet sergeant major to put you in my squad. He don't much like those of us that ain't high cotton. So's he'll be happy to put you in with the other North Alabama boys that make up our little group."

In his new squad, Caleb's life eased into a basic routine that he "learned by just degrees that my situation did not seem as dreadful as first I apprehended." The day started with muster and announcements. Then the boys marched a short distance to breakfast, known affectionately as "peas on a trencher," normally comprised of eggs and "ginned cotton" (grits). Then, they attended classes throughout the morning until a lunch of "piney woods rooters" (pork) and "hard tack." After lunch, they began work details until dinner. Dinner was followed by free time until final muster and taps.

Ridge's company of rural boys seemed to get most of the dirtier jobs like working the stables. But Caleb's entries seemed to indicate that the result was a strong emotional bond for the group that "asked no odds" (favors).

Hannah learned that the LaGrange Military Academy commandant was a local minister named Peabody Ross. As a "first year, Caleb stood behind two other rows of cadets in his squad of eighteen each morning as Reverend Ross passed among the cadets behind the cadet sergeant major. Ross acted more like a reverend school master than a military commandant. As a result, he never found fault with the cadets' uniforms or formations. Caleb wasn't inclined to military training and let his mind wander in the ranks. He dreamily watched the birds rise from the mist in the cool fall morning. This was his favorite time of the day. The morning's fog seemed to provide a security blanket for squirrels that scurried along the ground gathering breakfast before the heat of day burned off the fog, which protected them from the watchful gaze of hawks looking for a meal of their own.

"What's your name?" asked the headmaster, who suddenly stood before Caleb, shaking him from his trance.

"Caleb Rochester, sir," said Caleb meekly. His feeble response drew a glare from the cadet sergeant major, who found it quite un-soldierly.

"You're the new boy from the neighboring county, aren't you?" said the reverend. He wasn't known to stop in the formation and ask questions. As a result, the other cadets seemed to peer over to see what the commotion was all about. It was like Caleb had just emerged from a confessional after admitting some grievous sin.

"Yes, sir," was all Caleb could seem to reply. The minister stood in silence, appearing to wait for Caleb to elaborate. But instead he just stared ahead, hoping that the man would move on. Seeming to realize Caleb's discomfort, the minister just smiled and proceeded down the line.

Caleb had been told that the minister was more focused on making the cadets follow what he prescribed as proper Christian thought and behavior than supervising the day-to-day military drills. He was everything you'd expect in a minister with the exception of being unmarried.

After his review, the reverend made a few comments that constituted the morning announcements. He concluded by admonishing each student to study hard and be grateful for the day God made. As quickly as it started, it was over and they were released for breakfast.

"What did you do last night, kill somebody?" chided Ridge. "The commandant never asks questions of the boys in the ranks."

The other cadets surrounded Caleb and asked what was said. "All he asked was, 'Are you the new boy'?" responded Caleb defensively.

"Why you?" came the reply.

"Don't rightly know," answered Caleb honestly.

Breakfast conversation then turned to the normal gossip of all boys.

"Did you see how the headmaster was baited for widow? He had a crisp white shirt under that black dress coat," said a cadet.

"That's what he always wears," observed Ridge. "Leave the man alone."

There was a silence as the cadets seemed to search their brains for anything in the minister's character to spin into some conjecture, but there was none. So, the conversation turned to the shortcomings of other cadets.

It was true, the headmaster was always the same in personality and appearance. He always appeared in crisp white shirt, black coat and neatly cropped blond hair atop a tall frame. He never seemed to judge cadets too harshly unless they were caught "larking" (performing some prank) like taking a trusting young cadet "snipe hunting" (tricking the cadet to sit in the dark forest with a gunny sack, hitting two sticks together, in an attempt to attract and catch this mythical woodland creature). This type of behavior he considered the act of a "road agent" (criminal) against the innocent who should instead be shepherded as our "Lord and Savior Jesus Christ so aptly demonstrated." He likewise insured that there was always time for letters and writing each night. Pastoral vestments were reserved for Sunday mass.

Conversation slowed as Miss Kate rang the school bell, signaling that breakfast was over and they had to proceed to class. Caleb carried his wooden plate and tin cup to a wash basin in front of the slave. He was one of the few who said, "Thank you for breakfast, Miss Kate."

She returned an almost imperceptible curtsey.

Miss Kate completed all manner of tasks from cooking and cleaning to general administration. She would have been considered the equivalent of a church secretary and housemother had it not been for the fact that she was a slave. While some of the more aristocratic cadets from plantations avoided using her title and addressed her as Kate or worse, most cadets gave her the respect and affection she deserved as their caregiver.

Caleb noticed that Miss Kate seemed to keep her emotions hidden on her sundried but beautiful face. He had commented to Ridge, "She always smiles revealing a Godly soul, but her sullen eyes seem to hide an inner sorrow." She acted with dignity despite rude remarks by returning no objection but silent compliance. None of these remarks were made in the presence of the headmaster who quickly rebuked any such lack of manners. The headmaster also insured that there was never a shortage of help to assist her with her tasks— usually junior cadets who helped with the cooking and cleaning. In truth, cooking with Miss Kate was seen more like a joyful homecoming than a chore as she acted more like a mother preparing a family gathering. When not in the kitchen or cleaning the school, she tended the headmaster and lived in a small cabin between the smoke house and "summer kitchen" (a cabin for cooking to avoid the spread of fire). The winter kitchen was in the school's basement (on a hill with the lower level acting as the brick enclosed kitchen) that likewise served to heat the school. Life must have been good, because some cadets commented that she was becoming slightly pudgier as of late.

Where Miss Kate seemed a "saintly soul," the quartermaster, James Miller, who basically acted as a business manager, seemed to represent Lucifer himself.

"Put your back into it, or I'll stick my 'Arkansas toothpick' (knife) right up your spine," he yelled as Caleb's squad unloaded supplies.

"You can smell the stump liquor all over him," complained Caleb to Ridge.

"Just never you mind," admonished Ridge. "The sooner we get the wagons unloaded, the sooner we can be rid of this work detail."

All the while, the unkempt bear of a man barked insults at the cadets.

They in turn made quiet comments among themselves. "His hair seems more like a bird's nest than any human growth," commented one.

About this time, the headmaster walked by and heard the insults. When cadets looked the headmaster's way, he pretended to notice nothing and moved on, leaving them to their fate.

"Why don't the headmaster do something about that yamacraw?" asked Caleb.

"Either Miller's got some 'big bug' (important person) beholden to him or he's got something over the reverend," conjectured Ridge.

"Has anybody ever asked the reverend direct?"

"No," said Ridge, shaking his head. "He's even been told about Miller's thieving from the cadets, but all he says is that we should pray about whatever inner demons drive the man."

Every cadet knew that they were overcharged for sundries like soap and hard candy. But they learned to make purchases only when absolutely required.

The only other man at the Military Academy who was known to make threats to the cadets was Bobby Joe Swanson. He was a short man with sullen features who kept to his business. But he quickly left his grounds manager business when any cadet even glanced at his teenage daughter, Millie.

The first time Caleb saw her face, the entire world seemed to stop. It was as if the birds and trees became aware of their own shortcomings by comparison and chose to shrink into the silent landscape.

"Keep your eyes to yourself or I'll put a 'Davis boot' (poor man's boot that didn't distinguish between right and left) up your arse," said the little man to Caleb. With that, Millie demurely looked up and saw Caleb staring. At their eyes' meeting, Caleb became self-conscious and pretended to return to work.

"Chocolate box pretty, ain't she?" observed Ridge. The sight of her dark hair and deep brown eyes were permanently engraved on his brain like an etching in steel.

"You best keep away or Old Man Swanson will have you in a 'barrel shirt' (confined)" was the common threat delivered to any cadet showing an interest.

*****

Hannah rubbed her eyes, fatigued by deciphering the old script. She looked out the front window at the cotton mill blanketed in shadows. Its numerous windows seemed to stare back with eyes of black. Her mind instantly conjured images of murderers and rapists, both alive and dead, standing behind the glass waiting for her lights to dim. A cold shudder ran up her spine. She couldn't help but check the locks one more time. But it was getting late and she had to work the next day, so she retreated to the bedroom and pulled the covers up until only her nose and eyes were still visible.

Not far away, the strange little man watched Hannah's lights go out from his vantage point inside the cotton mill. His unkempt black hair atop an expensive dress shirt looked like the animal equivalent of a wolf in sheep's clothing. He edged backward, lest he be seen in the glow of the streetlamp illuminating the window. He thought to himself, *She's so smug in that little house. Her meddling with the grass and such is affecting my business, and I've got to do something to warn her off without her suspecting that I'm here. She's got to believe that the neighborhood's not safe for her.*

Chapter 7
Headaches of Life

The next morning, Hannah emerged to glistening grass atop wet ground from rain the night before. She stepped off the walkway onto the soggy turf, creating a sensation of sliding on the mud underneath. Hannah dreaded the workday to come where she had to inspect several worksites, knowing that mud would be everywhere, feebly covered by a labyrinth of board used as bridges. Luckily, this wasn't her first rodeo and she wore the equivalent of farm boots, which invariably conflicted with her dress pants and blouse. Some of the credit union's old guard could get away with jeans for such an occasion, but being junior *and* a woman, she was sensitive to avoid the appearance of being too liberal. That meant dealing with the splatters of mud on clothing later.

Hannah paused as she became aware of the birds busying themselves with seeking worms coming up for air. The sight of nature and the fresh, crisp air countered her mood. Maybe she would stop at the garage convenience store to see if the handsome proprietor was present.

A few minutes later, she pulled in front of a gas station pump and filled her truck's tank while casually glancing into the store. She saw him behind the counter through the large glass window. After topping off her truck, Hannah ventured inside and past the bananas, fruit cups, and coffee to retrieve a honey bun, its glistening sugar coating protected nicely by a factory-sealed wrapper. To wash it down, she made what she called her "preferred blend" of a large diet fountain drink mixed with a small blast of regular root beer for taste. She was normally an iced tea drinker but substituted a fountain drink on occasion.

Hannah placed the items on the counter and made another attempt at discussion with the handsome owner. Before she could say anything, he smiled and asked, "Are you on your way to work?"

Hannah was momentarily stunned. She had to answer a question rather than her normal process of mumbling a reflex response to a disinterested kid sporting an "I'm Scooter" nametag. His quick movement to scan and ring up the purchase made her slightly more confused before she finally stammered, "Yes, I guess so."

"You're not sure?" he asked with a smile.

"I just moved to Leigh Acres and am getting settled in," Hannah said, trying to sound confident but realizing she was giving her life story and didn't answer the question. "And, yes, um, I work at the credit union."

"I know," he countered.

Just then, a customer rushed in and interrupted, putting $20 on the counter. "Put that on pump three." He was followed by two more people equally rude in their requests without a hint of manners.

"Bless their hearts," he said, sliding the money into the drawer. For lack of a better idea, Hannah smiled and waved goodbye.

It had been a long day as Hannah finally pulled into her driveway. It started with an argument with a local contractor. She had attempted to explain politely that having plastic-encased bales of electrical wire on the job site floor didn't constitute finished wiring; that qualified for the next construction draw. Despite her attempt at diplomacy, he ended the conversation with, "Well, old Clyde Higgins at the credit union would do it. I'll ring him up."

Later that same day, Hannah was summoned to Clyde Higgins office where she was told that he had released the funds. He admonished Hannah to "learn how to treat their customers the 'right way.'" When she countered that the bank regulations were designed to avoid the real estate losses recently experienced by all banks and credit unions, including theirs, she was rebuffed with, "They had a way of doing things that the regulator need not know about."

Hannah was in a sour mood as she entered the house and dealt with the cats who she thought were not in tune with her feelings in any way. She sullenly opened a can of Hormel chili for herself. Luckily, she had shredded cheddar cheese in a bag, and crackers. While the number of ingredients was over her normal limit (one), the recipe was simple: heat chili in the microwave (after removing from can). Mix all three ingredients together. The cats saw the activity with an ever bigger can than their own and objected loudly with several choruses of "Yow!"

"This isn't for you. You'd be up all night after eating that." Hannah paused to think about how she was probably going to be up all night herself but shrugged it off. She would worry about that after enjoying dinner. She retreated with her steaming bowl to the porch.

Hannah knew that Lisa was working late, so she ate as she scanned the cotton mill across the street. Since it had rained the day before, there were muddy tire tracks across the now cut grass leading to the building. Unfortunately, she saw that the tracks served as a pointer to new graffiti. *So, I guess even rain serves as cover to buy drugs or their spray-painting activities,* she thought. After eating, she walked over to take a closer look at the graffiti and realized it was different than before. The former markings included "RIP Snake" and an elaborate five-pointed star followed by a rudimentary arrow. The new markings seemed almost random shapes and letters. Earl must have seen Hannah walk to the mill because he suddenly appeared at her side.

"I see the graffiti is back," he observed tersely.

"They seem very different this time," commented Hannah.

"They won't be different for long. I'll get the paint out of your shed and take care of them," he said, turning in the direction of her backyard.

"Wait," said Hannah, stopping him. "You sure that whoever did it won't be angry, like some local gang? Maybe I'm supposed to stay away."

"Not as angry as me. And besides, that's all the more reason for me to do it instead of you."

"I just can't sit and watch while you work," objected Hannah.

"I tell you what. You go to the Leigh Acres Library and find a book or read your journal. It will be a good diversion," said Earl, trying to guide her away from the graffiti.

Hannah resigned herself to letting Earl take care of it and walked to the little library just fifty yards away. There, she found one of the computers free and proceeded to log on. With graffiti on her mind, she decided to research what gangs, if any, were in the area and any unwritten rules regarding their markings. She found that numerous gangs with large concentrations were further south in Birmingham and Montgomery. However, rural areas, including North Alabama, had their fair share of biker clubs and hate groups, like the KKK and Arian Brotherhood. A review of their symbols indicated that the original markings were gang-related. The arrow next to the star designated that a gang was marking its territory. The "RIP Snake" was a salute to a fallen member, so named after a reptile—hopefully not by his mother.

The good news was that Hannah and Earl had painted over the symbols with simple paint versus placing an "X" over the markings. That indicated to any gang that it was not a sign of disrespect—but just a resident trying to spruce up the neighborhood.

The new markings didn't match normal gang symbols and were more of a mystery. They weren't related to a typical street artist who normally placed the name of a girlfriend or created a rudimentary work of art. So, they would require more thought. Somebody was making a statement, but what was it? The good news was that Hannah didn't seem to be in any real danger of retaliation.

Not wanting to rush Earl, Hannah opened the journal she brought from home and took up where she had left off.

*****

The teacher stood in front of Caleb's class pointing at the drawing of a floating keg from *English Gentleman's Magazine*, which featured articles of interest for "men of higher learning." It showed a floating bomb built by David Bushnell in the American Revolution. Bushnell had filled the keg with gunpowder and created a watch-work timing devise to ignite the explosive when it came near an enemy ship.

Caleb looked at the drawing as if they were looking at some fantastic technology beyond human imagination while the teacher explained that these bombs could be deployed to protect harbors from enemy encroachment by sea. Caleb was about to ask a question when his attention was drawn to Miss Kate, who waved him to the door. "Yes, Miss Kate?"

"Headmaster Ross has requested your presence in his office, Master Caleb," Miss Kate said with a smile. On the way, Caleb wondered if one of the boys from Montgomery had made a bad report to the headmaster that would be sent to his parents. His father would be deeply disappointed.

Caleb nervously entered the relatively modest but comfortable office. Roughhewn furniture filled the small area, with modest bookshelves surrounding the room. Each shelf displayed an assortment of books, mainly having to do with theology. Caleb was drawn to the books, some authors of which he recognized from Sunday school. But he knew not to linger because he was summoned for a reason.

"I was hoping to acquaint myself with how you're getting on. Is your squad receiving your fair share of nuts for you boys?" asked the headmaster, using slang. It was as if he was trying to put Caleb at ease by using a common cadet phrase referring to easy work assignments.

"We get our fair share, sir. When we don't get a plumb assignment, we work with infinite labor to do our duty." The truth was that they generally got the dirtier jobs like cleaning the stables while the squads from the more affluent areas got the plumb assignments like straightening classrooms. But complaining would only make matters worse. And besides, Caleb's squad drew a certain amount of pride that they did the harder jobs. It drew them closer together.

"I realize that the good jobs are as scarce as hen's teeth. But if you boys find otherwise, you tell me and I'll 'wake snakes' (loudly complain)."

"Yes, sir."

"How about your schoolin'? Is it coming natural to you?"

"I guess so, sir. It don't 'beat the Dutch' (seem nonsensical) or anything. I understand it just fine. But back home, I've always been good at books and such, when I could get them."

The headmaster then asked about his impressions of the school and his military duties.

"I don't care much for marching. But I don't need a piece of hay or straw to remind me the difference between my left and my right, or nothing," Caleb responded sincerely. Left and right weren't terms used in the country and some farm boys had to be taught marching by tying a piece of hay to one leg and straw to the other to learn the difference.

"I've seen you in chapel quite regularly. Is that because your parents told you so, or do you come for some other reason?"

"I do my nightly prayers recognizing each saint in-turn," answered Caleb. "Nobody told me so."

"I'm not so much interested in religious rules. I'm wondering more about your salvation. Do you turn to God in times of trouble?"

"I like God just fine and promise to turn to him rightly when the occasion calls for it."

The reverend then turned to talk of politics, which seemed an abrupt change. "What do you think about states' rights?"

"States have rights, just like the rest of us, I guess," answered Caleb pensively.

"Do you think the states have a right to make their own decision on the issue of slavery?"

"I don't know any slaves besides Miss Kate. It ain't been much of a botherment. But I don't like the idea that any owner could 'tump' (hit) her when the mood pleases them. So, I reckon not."

The headmaster didn't seem to entirely like that answer but agreed that he didn't much like the thought of anyone hurting Miss Kate either.

When Caleb returned to his barracks, he shared the meeting with Ridge.

"So, do you think he'll send a bad report to my paw?"

"Naw. He's a richous man and ain't done nothing to hurt any of the boys who all had a meeting just like it a month or so after they started. You just have to listen to his rigmarole and leave," said Ridge with a laugh.

"I was tempted to ask him about why he's so humbugged by that jackleg quartermaster. How can he just let Miller pad his pockets with our money for soap and such?"

The conversation continued with a focus on the quartermaster until Caleb and Ridge worked up enough frustration to develop a plan to gather evidence of Miller's "thievin'" that same night.

It was dark as they silently moved along the tree line. Each took great care to cover any lighter-colored clothing with their dark gray uniform jackets, lest they be seen in the moonlight.

After their earlier discussion, they had come to the realization that the headmaster wouldn't do anything about James Miller, no matter how many cadets reported his "thievin'." They reasoned that they needed hard proof. If the headmaster was confronted with that, he'd be forced to act. So, they hatched a plan to see if they could find some ledger showing what the students were charged versus what the quartermaster had entered in the books. Short of that, they would look at the supplies to see if they found anything suspicious; they knew not what.

So, they now found themselves hidden in a ditch a few yards from the supply barn containing Miller's meager records on payments and inventory. But, there was a problem.

"What's he still doing in there?" whispered Caleb.

"He must have gotten some jugs of John Barleycorn in with the supply shipment. He and the driver seem to be whooping it up," answered Ridge.

"Great, that's all we need. Two scalawags with Arkansas toothpicks with a keg of beer. They'll be mollygrubbing about like madmen."

"Don't fret now. When we spy him going to home, we'll make our way in," counseled Ridge.

The two sat in silence as the libations turned ugly. The driver stormed out, leaving the quartermaster to sulk in his chair behind the semblance of a counter where he normally dispensed cadet purchases. The boys watched as the quartermaster went in and out of the entrance, grumbling to himself while he took sporadic swigs from his jug. The irony was that alcohol was strictly forbidden on academy grounds by order of the teetotaling headmaster. Nevertheless, something had the quartermaster doubly agitated beyond his normal bad temperament.

After a while, Miller finally retreated home.

"See, I told you," whispered a victorious Ridge.

"Look at him zigzagging like a Virginia fence," chuckled Caleb.

Caleb was about to get up when Ridge held him back. "Let's wait until he gets to the 'macadam' (loose stone) trail leading to his cabin. That way we know he's gone for sure."

The boys watched Miller seem to replay an argument with an unknown assailant all the way home. Then, Ridge gave the signal and they made their way to the barn door. Unfortunately, it was secured with a large rusty padlock. After quietly making their way around the building looking for an opening, they settled on climbing a line threaded through a block and tackle flowing down from the upper loft. As luck would have it, the line was still tethered to a net containing two fully laden barrels sufficient to counterbalance their weight. So after much effort, they climbed the rope to the loft and made their way to the lower-level counter where Caleb loudly knocked over a tin bucket.

"Quiet now," admonished Ridge.

"Sorry."

They lit a gas lamp on the lowest setting and began reading the journal. Here's an entry for the goober peas I bought last week," observed Ridge, who raced his finger to the amount paid. "That's the amount, all right."

"Is that the handful you showed me?" asked Caleb.

"Yes," confirmed Ridge.

"Maybe that's how he's cheating the school," said Caleb, tracing his finger down the left side of all the entries. "He never writes how much he sold. I bought soap last week and he only gave me a half bar, saying that they was in short supply. But he just wrote 'soap' next to what I paid—that should have been for a full bar."

They were both silent for a minute, then Ridge said the obvious. "So we can't prove anything with this."

"We have to see if there's some secret stash of supplies that he's skimmed off the top for delivery to some other paying customer," concluded Caleb.

"What good will that do?" asked Ridge.

Caleb thought for a moment. "If we know where it is, maybe we can mark it somehow and trace where it goes?"

"I guess," said a dubious Ridge. "I expect it's better than nothing."

They began to quietly search when they heard the quartermaster appear and yell, "Who's there?" They doused the lamp and scurried toward the loft opening and were halfway down the line when the quartermaster tried pulling it back up with Caleb still astride. Caleb jumped and turned his ankle, limping to the tree line in escape.

The next day, all the cadets were under the watchful eye of the quartermaster. In formation, Caleb did his best to disguise his limp when passing the quartermaster's gaze. But it caught the notice of the cadet sergeant major. After dismissing the regiment, he stopped Caleb.

"Cadet Rochester. Why ain't you reported to 'Company Q' (sick call) to see the doctor?"

Caleb was acutely aware that the quartermaster was staring from the edge of the parade grounds.

"It's nothing, sir. Just kicked by a brevet horse in the stables."

"I saw it," confirmed Ridge as he walked between the senior cadet and his squad. "It twerent nothing. Besides, Doctor Fosburgh ain't do to visit for another day."

"So, see Miss Kate then," said the cadet sergeant major, exercising his authority.

"Yes, sir," replied Ridge and Caleb in unison.

Miss Kate was accustomed to treating minor ailments and sprains with local remedies of her own. In truth, half the treatments administered were just compassion from the woman who many of the boys saw as a substitute mother. Caleb found Miss Kate in the summer kitchen in the first stages of cutting vegetables for lunch.

"Sorry to bother you, Miss Kate. But, the cadet sergeant major says I have to see you about my leg."

"Just sit yourself down. I have just the remedy you need."

"What is it made of, Miss Kate?" asked Caleb, more out of curiosity than concern. "I always help my grandma mix remedies. She knows I have an interest in healing and such."

"Oh, this and that," replied Miss Kate evasively. "Let me go fetch it."

Caleb winced as he limped to a bench. Just then, the headmaster came in through the side door and said, "Darling?"

Seeing Caleb, he jumped, not expecting to see any cadets in the vicinity, then stammered, "I was looking for Miss Kate—that little 'darlin''—about school business.

Caleb was equally startled and jumped himself. "She went to fetch some medicine, sir."

The headmaster then mumbled something about his concern but needed to leave for an urgent matter. Caleb was left standing in confusion about the strange incident.

*****

Hannah turned from the journal and tried to pronounce "darlin'" with an elongated drawl at the front to differentiate it from "darling." It sounded strange when she did it, but she got the ruse.

*****

Later that day there was new excitement at the academy.

"What's going on?" asked Caleb to a passing cadet as he returned from Miss Kate's care.

"There's fixin' to be war!"

Caleb followed the cadet to the front of the school, where others were gathered around a carriage. Within just another minute, all cadets were there including Bull and his two toadies, who pushed their way to the front.

The headmaster conferred with the messenger, then addressed the little crowd. "I've just received word from the Alabama Secession Convention. The state of Alabama has voted to overthrow the federal constitution. As a result, Alabama ain't no longer part of no federal country. The state will send a delegation to work with the other states to create a confederacy of likeminded folks with equal rights for each."

Finished, the headmaster was surrounded by excited cadets. Caleb, Ridge, and others from the northern counties stayed behind.

"It happened like my paw said it would," lamented another member of the squad named Tyler.

"Mine, too," confirmed another.

"My paw wrote last week that Winston County was going to send a schoolteacher, Charles Sheats, who was going to say that we have no cause to leave the Union. I wonder what happened to him?" asked Caleb.

"Thrown in jail, I expect," complained Ridge.

*****

Hannah used her smartphone to do some quick research on Sheats. He was in fact arrested, but released to return home. There, he attempted to form a group to keep the county out of the war on the grounds that nobody in the area owned slaves. It resulted in a lengthier arrest. Returning to the journal, the drama began again.

*****

"I'm likeminded with that feller," admitted Caleb.

"I am also," said Ridge. "Once I saw a slave man punished in a hot box. No man nor beast should be treated that way. Besides, back home, you are paid proper for workin' a man's land."

"Well, we better all keep quiet about it or we'll be put in a hot box and that ain't no lie," said another.

They all agreed and quickly disbursed, lest they draw more attention.

Caleb retreated to his bunk to ponder the situation. He himself had a stronger allegiance to the Union than most folks because of his grandfather's service in the American Revolution. The other cadets knew that Caleb's family had helped settle North Alabama, but Caleb never mentioned that his granddad was from the upper east. When Caleb was a "porch baby" and not allowed to venture into the yard, his grandfather began entertaining him by recounting his time as a Patriot.

As the years went by, their bond grew and Caleb's grandfather recounted in more detail what drove him to become a Continental soldier when most of his neighbors supported the crown. He explained that when he was a boy, the family took pride in being from Virginia, not far from the oldest settlement at Jamestown. Successive generations migrated further north to the outer settlements in the Connecticut Valley, where they helped to tame the area. One day, when Caleb's grandfather and great uncle were transporting "cracker poles" (fishing poles) to their fishing shack on the Connecticut River, their rowboat was stopped by a British patrol searching for Patriot smugglers. The British threw their equipment and supplies over the side for sport and warned them that if they didn't turn in any Yankees supplying Washington's army, they would be met with a cat o' nine tails. His grandfather and his brother later watched an innocent sloop try to outrun the British in-shore squadron to evade confiscation of their cargo. The little schooner was quickly destroyed by a devastating broadside.

Shortly thereafter, Caleb's grandfather traveled southward to join the Virginia Continental Line, while his brother signed on a colonial supply ship evading the British from a port out of reach in Bermuda. The two survived the war, and successive generations kept in contact despite the ocean that separated America and the little island nation in the mid-Atlantic.

Caleb sat for hours while his grandfather regaled him with stories recounting his time as a private in Captain John Cunningham's Company of Virginia troops. Caleb begged him to repeat the stories where they fought side by side with the Green Mountain Boys. It was this association with the Southern farmers that led to his grandfather's ultimate move south to the Alabama territory.

Caleb considered himself linked to the creation of the United States and the people his grandfather served with, including the Green Mountain Boys. He saw the secessionists from the lower Alabama plantations as out for personal wealth, glory, and the preservation of slavery at the expense of the other American farmers. But, like the Patriots in the American Revolution, there was tension and danger among Alabamians and the divided cadets. Caleb and his squad were definitely outnumbered and would have to keep their thoughts to themselves. Apparently, the same discussion was going on all around—especially back home as indicated by his father's letter that said "most folks see secession as a way to start a plantation owner's war." Small farmers feared their crops would be confiscated for the army, while the plantations would keep their cotton and crops for themselves.

The next day, Caleb stood at attention in formation as a one-star flag was raised.

"Hand, salute," ordered the cadet sergeant major. Followed by "Ready, too."

Caleb and the other cadets snapped a salute out of reflex and dropped it on the second command. Caleb was sickened by having to salute a flag other than the Union Jack. The headmaster stood in front of the formation and said, "The new flag signifies that the single star of Alabama now flies alone. We are no longer part of the United States. In the coming weeks and months, a new flag may follow with more stars as our delegates meet. You're dismissed."

As they were released from muster, the other squads surrounded the boys from the northern counties. Bull now faced Ridge.

"Are you boys loyal to the new Alabama?"

Not being one to back down, Ridge replied, "We're loyal to our kin. And our kin are from 'bama, ain't they? Their druthers are our ruthers. So, we do what they say."

Knowing that the families in the northern counties were against secession, Ridge's comments were taken badly. Bull threw the first punch, followed by many more from the other squads. Caleb took a punch to the stomach as he tried to help Ridge, but managed to land a couple punches in return. Luckily, the headmaster ran back, yelling for everyone to stop. When they did, he asked, "Who started the fight?"

Bull and his entourage pointed to Caleb and Ridge.

"You two come with me. The rest of you boys, back to your barracks."

Caleb and Ridge followed the headmaster to his little office.

"Now, boys, 'acknowledge the corn' (tell the plain truth). Nothing will happen to you if you tell me the truth," said the headmaster in a kindly tone.

Ridge looked at Caleb as if to say, *Should we trust him?*

Caleb looked back with a shrug.

So, Ridge spoke, "the corn is that we don't see why we have to fight a plantation owner's war. If'n it comes to it, we'll do our duty. But it ain't clear what that duty is."

The headmaster sat silently, contemplating Ridge's words. The he finally said, "You'll have to choose who to fight for soon enough. But it would be better to keep your thoughts to yourself. Otherwise, you might get fighting before you can ever make it to a battlefield. Go back to your barracks and tell your squad to keep to themselves, no matter who tries to raise their temper."

So, Caleb and Ridge made their way back to the barracks. School just became a place of great danger.

*****

Hannah put down the journal once again. Her stomach was in knots and she found herself worrying about the boys. She had to remind herself that they had been dead 150 years and let it go.

Bert noticed her pause from reading and subtly pointed toward the clock. It was long-past closing time for the little library.

"I'm so sorry, Bert," she said, closing the journal.

"I'm just glad that you found something of value in that old vault," he said, chuckling at his own joke.

After exchanging a few more pleasantries, Bert locked up while Hannah made it home in the dark. Earl had long since finished painting over the new graffiti and gone home himself. Now, Hannah would have to see if her internet research was correct. If not, she was going to have a war of her own.

Chapter 8
The Ruins

Hannah's construction inspections took her near the LaGrange Military Academy around lunchtime, so she decided to walk the ruins. Just a couple weeks since her visit for the July 4th skirmish, she now saw the place in a totally different light. The last time she was here, she focused on cooking and socializing with the living with little care regarding the school ruins that served more as a backdrop than anything else. Now, the school's stone walls lay like a long-deceased man in a graveyard. The sun shone on his craggy face. The once proud body seemed to lay in a crumbled mess with walls half their original height of brick still standing along with an old chimney at either end. The inside reflected the life that had once abounded inside with neatly cut grass and large window openings from which to gaze at the surrounding grounds. What was left stood in spite of itself, defying gravity in its precarious way.

Hannah munched on her bologna sandwich on white bread, her all-time favorite combination. She absentmindedly ate as she walked, envisioning a group of cadets scrambling out of the building to find their prearranged spot in the ranks, lest they be punished for their tardiness. Then, they stood at attention as a crisp wind swept the hillside up to the school. She imagined the sight of Caleb and Ridge in uncomfortable wool jackets with rough edges that made then squirm impatiently as the headmaster waded through the day's tedious business.

Hannah's gaze moved around the now-empty perimeter as she wondered where the supply shed had been or the cabin housing the groundskeeper and his daughter Millie. She felt some pangs of worry but then reasoned that it was foolish to think such things. They were all long dead and a distant memory—if only in her mind.

Out of the corner of her eye, she saw a figure and turned just as he disappeared around the far wall.

"Can I help you?" she said, trying to get his attention as she scurried to follow. As Hannah rounded the corner, there was nothing there. She went the length of the wall at a trot to round the back and saw nothing. A cold chill went up her spine.

Hannah stood dumbfounded when a hand touched her shoulder. "Did Lisa and Earl send you up here to check on me?" asked EJ.

Hannah jumped a foot at the touch. "So, that was you rounding the corner?" asked Hannah.

"No," said EJ quizzically. "I heard you yell and saw you running around the building. I came out from inside a shed."

"So, you didn't see that other man?" stammered Hannah

"No. But don't let it worry you. You ain't the first to swear they seen some ghostly apparition," said EJ matter-of-factly.

"Have you ever seen anything?" asked Hannah, embarrassed.

"I think I see something from time to time. But I always chalk it up to being on the mountain too long."

They stood in silence for a moment as Hannah tried to shake off the feeling of being watched. "I guess it was nothing. Maybe reading those school journals you arranged are taking their toll," confided Hannah.

"So, you're enjoying them? I assumed you'd find some reference to supplies or other school business and return them after a couple days," observed a surprised EJ.

"You would probably have been right if I hadn't found the personal diary of a cadet in that leather pouch at the bottom," observed Hannah.

"Really? I've been through those documents a couple, three times and never saw no leather pouch," said a dubious EJ.

"Really," answered Hannah emphatically. "It was at the bottom with a wax seal on it."

"In a pouch you say," said EJ, shaking his head. "I can't believe I missed that."

Hannah said nothing in return. It appeared that the diary was as much a mystery as the apparition she just chased.

"Well," said Hannah finally, "I best be getting back to work." With that, they went their separate ways. Hannah glanced back more than once on the way to her car, trying to shake off her feeling of dread.

That night, Hannah confided in Lisa about her strange experience.

"Yes, I already heard about it," responded Lisa. "EJ told Earl that he was concerned about you."

"He also said that other people had seen them, including himself," responded Hannah hopefully.

"I hate to tell you, but he was just being nice."

"I was afraid of that," groaned Hannah.

"I know you're a little frightened, but you never said anything about actually seeing a ghost," said Lisa, now touching Hannah's arm for emphasis. "You don't actually believe you're seeing one, do you?"

"No, I guess not," answered Hannah pensively.

"Do you think the journal's getting to you?"

"No. I know they're long dead and in the grave. I just want to know what happened to them," answered Hannah with more authority.

"Okay, that's fair. Tell me more about the journal. What's the latest development?"

"Well," said Hannah. "The cadets from near here, mainly Winston County, are continuing to have a rough time of it." Hannah went on to explain their situation getting worse with the secession movement pitting neighbor against neighbor, and rich against poor. Almost to drive home the point, a freight train blew its whistle three long blasts as it approached the downtown train crossing. It then blew it another three times as it approached the next crossing a quarter mile further as it sped at near full speed. The noise was almost ear-splitting, and Leigh Acres residents knew to stop talking or trying to hear the TV when it went through. In wealthier towns and suburbs, the trains slowed to a crawl and weren't allowed to blow their whistle, disturbing residents. Even the engine seemed to know that there were haves and have-nots.

"I suppose," nodded Lisa. "It's the same with people today who're divided on issues from economics to politics. Looking back, there's no reason to believe people weren't the same back then. I'm a little surprised, though, given the amount of pride people take in the Confederacy and their membership groups: Sons and Daughters of the Confederacy. I don't think I ever recall anybody ever saying their kin was opposed to the war. They all make out like they almost singlehandedly won the war."

"Did I ever tell you about my great-great-grandfather who fought at Bunker Hill?" asked Hannah

"No," said Lisa in surprise.

"He was famous for wrapping his rifle in a blanket and yelling, 'Don't shoot, you'll hit the baby.'" She immediately followed with an imitation of a drummer doing a vaudevillian rim shot, in a time well before TV laugh tracks.

"I don't think I'd put that in your application to one of those groups," chuckled Lisa, "*or* quit your day job."

After a little more conversation, Earl sped by on his way home from a late job and Lisa left. Hannah, like every other night of late, opened the journal and the scenes of academy life unfolded before her.

*****

Caleb was shaken awake in his bunk. He instinctively guarded his face, waiting for a punch.

"Stand down," said Ridge. "It's just me and a couple of the boys. Get up."

"Where we going?"

"We've been ordered on a work detail."

"At this hour?" objected Caleb.

"Yes. A wagon just came in from town. Maybe there's something in it they don't want people to see."

Caleb and the others in his squad rubbed their eyes as they made their way to the supply barn. Once there, Caleb was handed a supply list.

"Move anything on the list marked with an X to the borouche carriage. The farmer is going to store it for the school. Move the rest to the supply barn. I have to conduct a little business with the driver," said Miller, the quartermaster.

"But why? There's plenty of room if we stack it real careful," croaked Ridge.

"Just do as you're told. I don't have to explain myself to some goober digger."

Caleb and Ridge looked at the ornate passenger carriage. "Look at that knight of the ribbons over there with that gold-leafed carriage. That shipment ain't going to no farm," said Ridge.

"I'll try to remember the goods that go in the carriage as best I can. We can write it down later," whispered Caleb. The boys set to work before wearily returning to bed.

The next morning at formation, the headmaster read the new conscription laws, which trumped any thoughts of a dishonest quartermaster. The cadets listened in earnest to hear who had to go and who got to stay. As the headmaster read through the details, it was clear that the laws favored cadets who came from high cotton.

"Fourth, any family that owns a factory or other industry that supplies the Confederate Army is exempt from service. Lastly, the Twenty Negro Law states that if you are the owner or overseer of a plantation with more than twenty Negro slaves, you are exempt from service in the Confederate Army. That is all."

*****

Hannah looked it up on her smartphone and saw that the Twenty Negro Law was extremely controversial to most Southerners. One general, D. H. Hill, was quoted as saying that those exercising the exemption were actually "masters of an infinite amount of cowardice." Caleb's squad mates apparently agreed.

*****

Caleb, Ridge, and a couple of other cadets huddled together. "It's pretty clear that most of the cadets from plantations, and silver spoon boys from merchant families, don't have to go off and get killed," commented one.

"I heard Bull say that his paw arranged for him to be apprenticed as an apothecary to receive a medical supplier exemption," said Ridge with some disgust. "That boy couldn't mix two glasses of water without getting it wrong. With what your grandma taught you about healing and your book smarts, that should be you, Caleb."

"It's clear that we farm boys have to do the fighting," responded Caleb.

They noticed the other squads look their way and decided to move on lest they create another confrontation. Those with an exemption were raring to show their dedication to the cause by picking a fight with anyone who might be seen as sympathetic to the North. A little while later, two cadets from Caleb's squad were cornered while working in the kitchen by four such boys.

"You boys are good at making johnnycakes. Back home, only slave boys and their mommas do that. Is your momma a slave, boy?"

The reply came in the form of a bowl being pushed in the face of the lead boy, followed by fists. Within seconds, boys rushed to the doors to watch the fight. Miss Kate tried to intervene and was pushed to the ground by the lead attacker. This galvanized those on the sidelines who pushed the "hard case" (bully) out of the room and helped Miss Kate to her feet. They then turned their wrath on the carriage trade boys who had started the fight. These boys quickly retreated while a small group remained to help salvage what was left for breakfast.

Caleb and Ridge heard about the scuffle and rushed to the aid of their squad members just as it ended.

"You boys all right?" asked Ridge and Caleb, helping their two squad members to their feet.

"Yep. We got in a few shots to those flickers."

Miss Kate quietly cried as she saw all the morning's work ruined on the floor.

Ridge turned to her. "Don't fret, Miss Kate. We'll fetch some embalmed beef (corned beef) and hard tack from the supply barn. It don't need no cooking. It will feed the boys just fine, you watch."

A little while later, breakfast was tense as the cadets grudgingly ate their corned beef on a cracker instead of their normal hot meal. The headmaster made a long speech about loving one another and recognizing everyone's differences.

"And the apostles came from all walks of life, but were united in their love of Jesus. Follow their example lest you be seen as a Sadducee or Pharisee who persecuted our savior." The reverend's words fell on deaf ears. It didn't help that he received an exemption from conscription due to being a member of the clergy. This wasn't over yet.

*****

Hannah looked up as her grandfather clock struck twelve times. It made her think about earlier when she saw the apparition at the school, something that Southerners would call a "haint." She tried to put it out of her mind and turned off the light for bed. As usual, she stopped to look across the street at the cotton mill. She tried to shake the feeling of vulnerability resulting from her removal of the gang symbols by reminding herself that Earl and Lisa were literally a shout away. So, she checked the doors yet again and went to bed. Little did she know that her imagination wasn't that far off the mark.

The strange little man's knuckles were white from clenching his fist too hard as he watched from the mill's window. His hunched form exuded silent rage like acid burning. He had tried to *warn that woman off* with fake gang symbols to no effect. Now he needed another way to make her think twice about moving here and three times about moving back. The alternative was risking discovery of the family business that began before the Civil War. Great Grandad had started it by reselling moonshine acquired from the mountain folk. During the war, things became more difficult when his suppliers were conscripted into the Confederate Army. Luckily, smuggling had become rampant out of Bermuda. There, supply ships offloaded cargo in international waters out of reach of the blockading Union Navy in a process similar to that employed by the Patriots a century before. The supplies, like munitions and medicine, were transferred onto smaller blockade runners who could generally outrun the Union Navy and Revenue Cutter Service (later renamed the Coast Guard). Great Grandad saw a way of making money and appearing to support the southern cause by likewise supplying moonshine repackaged as medicinal alcohol to the Confederate Army. The secret family business exploded from there.

That woman obviously wasn't moved by his new gang symbol lookalikes. He'd have to think of something less subtle. He wasn't going to lose money because of an outsider, or worse, go to jail. The more he thought about it, the angrier he got.

Chapter 9
The Crush

After work the next day, Hannah knew not to eat or pick up the journal. Lisa had decided Hannah needed time away from home. Lisa announced that Hannah was coming to the Colbert County High School (containing Leigh Acres) football game with her and Earl. Hannah now sat in the stadium watching the Colbert County Indians play the Florence Falcons in their homecoming game. Sitting next to her was an unexpected blind date. Lisa had brought him along hoping that Ralph and Hannah would hit it off. The problem was, Ralph was screaming at the top of his lungs with each play, generally insulting the parentage of the referees.

Compounding the issue, Hannah had no interest in football. She was a hardcore history geek. The only player she knew in any detail was Roy Riegels, and then, only because she had heard him referred to more than once by Christian speakers. They recounted an event at a Rose bowl game between the University of California Golden Bears and the Georgia Tech Yellow Jackets. The incident happened midway into the second quarter where Riegels recovered a fumble near Georgia Tech's end zone, which would have been an easy score. However, Riegels got turned around and ran seventy yards in the wrong direction only to be tackled by his own players just before reaching the wrong end zone in a famous clip replayed thousands of times through the decades. What made the event noteworthy was the fact that Riegels returned to the field despite the humiliation and played a stellar second half. Inspirational speakers turned the clip and aftermath into a message about recovering from adversity.

Hannah thought about trying to share the story with her would-be date. She then rejected the thought after he spilled his beer on her for the third time. It wouldn't have been so bad, but beer wasn't allowed in the stadium and he had managed to smuggle in a six-pack.

After the game, Hannah managed to dodge overtures for a real date and make her way home. Luckily, like everything else in Leigh Acres, the high school was only two blocks from home.

A while later, Lisa arrived and joined Hannah on the porch.

"Sorry about that," said Lisa. "I had no idea he was like that. All I knew was that he was 'fun-loving.'"

"No problem, Lisa," replied Hannah. "It was a nice thought, but I think I'll continue with my approach."

"Exactly what approach is that?" asked Lisa.

"The approach where I avoid guys with more testosterone than a Marine rifle company."

After Lisa's brief apology explaining that she thought Hannah needed a distraction, she scurried home.

Hannah contemplated another night at home reading a dead cadet's musings across from a spooky mill. She decided that a change of venue was in order. She contemplated, and immediately dismissed, the thought of going to a bar. The only other place open at this hour was the university library. A room full of books was very much her style. So, within 20 minutes, she found herself at the large library asking for a visitor pass.

"I'm sorry, ma'am. We don't give visitor passes after 9:00 p.m.," said the young man.

"I understand," said Hannah, thinking, *What a perfect end to a perfect day.*

Just as Hannah was turning to leave, she caught an unexpected break.

"It's okay. I'll take responsibility. Please issue a pass. I'd do it myself, but I have to prepare for a morning talk," said a handsome man who had exited an office on route to an exit.

"Who was that masked man?" asked Hannah, who received only a strange look in return. Obviously, any reference to the Lone Ranger was lost on the collegiate, who was too young for the original series. On further thought, he was probably too young for the movie remake with Johnny Depp, which made Hannah feel even older.

"That's the new library administrator. So, we're cool," the student said with a shrug.

A few minutes later, Hannah made her way through the turnstiles to a long mahogany table with students interspersed every few feet. Each looked miserable, surrounded by papers with notes and formulas. Hannah smiled, thinking that she didn't miss the grind of tests and classes. She could read for enjoyment.

The journal began again as if continuing a movie in a DVD player. But this time, there was a new character.

*****

Caleb was summoned to the summer kitchen. It wasn't his turn to work and he was a little confused why there was a change in work assignments.

"Good afternoon, Miss Kate," he said with the lack of enthusiasm of a cadet appearing for work. Then he immediately became self-conscious when he saw that it was just himself, Miss Kate, and Millie, the grounds manager's beautiful daughter.

"You come right over here, Master Caleb," said Miss Kate, ushering him to a large wooden tub full of dirty dishes beside Millie. "I have to fetch some food for morning. So, you just get acquainted."

There was an awkward silence as Caleb reached into the water to retrieve a dish. Then, Caleb cleared his throat and croaked, "How are you, Miss Millie?"

"Fine," came the single-word response. She looked down at the tub while she worked.

Caleb became more nervous and tried to fill the silence by talking about how he helped his mother in the kitchen at home. He hoped that Millie would fancy his conversation. But, he ended his flurry of words with, "Did you help your momma?" As soon as he said it, he knew it was a mistake. Everyone at the military academy knew that Millie lived alone with her father. There were several rumors about her mother's fate, from death in childbirth to having run off with a salesman.

"I didn't know my mother," came the shy response.

"I'm sorry, Miss Millie. I didn't mean nothing by it. I was just jawing too much like an old hen."

"You ain't so much like the other boys," said Millie, who seemed to catch herself trying not to make offense, and added, "I mean, you seem more like me."

Caleb didn't see her much like himself at all. She was more like the perfect beauties drawn in a catalogue. He was about to answer when her paw entered the room.

"Where's that woman gone, leaving you two here like this?" he asked gruffly.

"She just run to fetch something, Mr. Swanson," stuttered Caleb defensively. In truth, he had no idea where she was and was just dragging out his chore to spend time with Millie.

Swanson then grabbed Millie and left. Caleb then made his way back to the barracks, hoping that he hadn't gotten Millie in trouble. He thought he could hear yelling in the distance as if coming from behind their cabin wall. But then, he thought better "to solace my mind" and assumed it was just the wind talking "to taunt my fears." He sulked the rest of the day.

Caleb's distress continued after he received a letter from home. His paw wrote that almost two-thirds of Winston County thought that secession was illegal and planned to refuse conscription. The farmers comprised the majority of federal sympathizers while the people of some economic standing, which were relatively few in the county, went firmly for the Confederacy.

His paw wrote: "Some are calling for us to declare the free state of Winston. But a home guard has formed to stop such talk. They operate after dark and we have to keep our wits about us. One farm was already burnt to the ground. You best stay away and focus on your studies as long as you can."

He talked to other squad mates who received similar letters.

"I'm fer going home. Nobody threatens my kin."

"But what about the treasury script paid by our kin for our schoolin'? How we gonna pay them back if we leave? We'll never become well situated unless we graduate," asked another.

"If'n we stay, we'll get drug off to the Confederate Army to help the very people that are threatening our kin," concluded Caleb.

"What does the headmaster say? How close are we to being conscripted?" asked a short, mousy cadet from Limestone County, very similar to Winston.

"I dunno. They say he's been offered some missionary post in Africa by the American Missionary Association and plans to take Miss Kate," answered another cadet from Franklin County, also in North Alabama.

"That ain't nothing but ugly canard," rebuked Ridge.

*****

Hannah was confused by the comment. Was it ugly because it involved taking Miss Kate? Or some other reason. Hannah looked up the American Missionary Association and found that it was an abolitionist group that evolved from a committee created to defend African slaves. The slaves in question had taken over their slave ship *Amistad* en route to Cuba. Hannah read with interest about the mutiny. In short, the mutineers (the slaves) spared the navigator in hopes of returning home. Unfortunately, he sailed northward until the ship was seized by the US Navy, which towed it into New London, Connecticut, where slavery was legal. The slaves were tried in court. At stake was their freedom or being sent to Cuba as slaves. Oddly enough, while slavery was legal in Cuba, the importation of African slaves was not. Therefore, the judge, and subsequently the US Supreme Court, ruled that the slaves were the subjects of an illegal kidnapping and freed.

Hannah contemplated the implications for the headmaster. The truth of the rumor seemed unlikely given his support of secession. While some Americans argued that the Civil War was all about states' rights and had nothing to do with slavery, most believed that slavery was the primary driver due to economics. The minister was clearly in favor of slavery, yet, he seemed a good Christian in other respects, which we assume, at least today, precludes human ownership. She wondered if there were other forces at work to discredit the man, but that would have to wait for another day. The library announced that it was closing in 15 minutes, and she didn't want to abuse her newly acquired visitor pass.

Chapter 10
The Pastor

It was Sunday morning and Hannah decided to go to church. She had become a Christian in college when friends joined a campus ministry organization. It led to a two-week mission trip to a Philippine orphanage. But given that her happiest experience of the trip was finding a fast food restaurant on the trip home, she decided she wasn't missionary material. After that, she limited her mission activities to writing a check.

Since coming to Leigh Acres, Hannah put off visiting any of the small local churches, fearing that each would be "family central." In a large urban church, she found it easy to locate a spot in the crowd relatively unnoticed or locate where the singles congregated. But her only experience at a country church found her wedged next to a large family that ultimately asked her to move to another seat when another member arrived.

Today she entered the local Presbyterian Church thinking that it would be small, yet structured enough to avoid extensive questions from members asking, "Where's your husband? Do you have kids?"

While they were well meaning, she still had no desire to create short answers that sounded like she had to defend herself.

This morning, she climbed the wide brick steps that led into the vestibule and then into the main sanctuary. The room was dimly lit with votive candles neatly arranged in a small grouping on the right, which caused light to dance on the ceiling from the slightly moving flames. Their scent mixed with the truly Anglican smell of polish and musty prayer books.

On the left was a door leading to a little vestry. Out of reflex, Hannah scanned for any signs indicating restrooms. She didn't see anything. In the North, church basements were easily accessible and invariably housed the porcelain-covered rooms if you needed to make a quick pit stop before a long service. In the South, the lack of basements made finding the lavatories more of a mystery, usually requiring an awkward question to a member.

About ten people sat sporadically in groups counting from one to three. Hannah unobtrusively slid into a pew and sat waiting for the bulk of people to arrive. When the mass started, the church was just a quarter full, leaving enough room for comfort with relative distance to avoid questions if they arose.

Given the small size of the church, Hannah expected a pastor of advanced years serving at his final parish or a very young pastor on his first stop from seminary. The pastor entered and Hannah was surprised to see a man in his mid-forties. He was strangely similar to the description of Caleb's reverend headmaster at LaGrange Military Academy apart from neatly cut brown hair and a muscular frame. More importantly, he was "the masked man" from the night before who authorized her visitor pass. The "morning talk" to which he referred was obviously his sermon.

The order of service was efficient given that it had been executed with little change since the Protestant Reformation. The part-time pastor focused on the teaching of Frederick Denison Maurice, which took Hannah by surprise. Hannah was a hardcore history buff. She actually knew this particular figure, who started a movement to educate and provide healthcare for impoverished families and their children during the British industrial revolution. He reasoned that they should become healthy and literate if for no other reason than to read the Bible. For that, he was branded a "Christian Socialist" who would ruin the country's economy by depriving factories of cheap child labor. This particular sermon didn't address that part of his work but focused on his thoughts relative to baptism. However, the fact that the minister even knew of the foreign pre-Civil War social engineer was something in his favor. The sermon was directly related to the readings and took about ten minutes. Hannah rated the sermon itself as unusually insightful and well done—especially given the size of the church.

As the service ended, the minister and altar attendants retreated down the center aisle to the church entrance to meet people on their way out. Hannah normally skirted around the invariable bottleneck, but today's little group made meeting the pastor inevitable. When normally confronted with the pastor, she would say, "nice sermon," whether she liked it or not. Hannah was renowned for having a hundred thoughts on a subject but having no ability or inclination to verbalize them. As a result, she always defaulted instead to some meaningless idiom that got her through the social interaction without ever displaying her opinion. So, she was seen as pleasant and a bit of a mystery, but little more. In contrast, Hannah herself found it odd that the people who actually pontificated on their thoughts generally had nothing of value to say. To her credit, at least she didn't fall into that category.

"Hi, I'm Mike Shackley," the pastor said, extending his hand. Hannah considered that a positive sign because he didn't use his formal title, which she always felt put the person slightly above the professionally untitled like herself.

"I'm Hannah. We sort of met at the library last night when you authorized a visitor pass. I live up the street and just moved to town for a job at the credit union."

"I'm glad. I just moved here for the university myself, which I guess you already know. I also have a seminary degree so I preach here part-time, given the church's limited size." Then he looked slightly uncomfortable with all the parishioner eyes straining to see who the new unmarried pastor was talking to at such length.

About that time, the next person in line interjected a brief greeting as if to say, "It's my turn," then launched into a question about some church business.

So, Hannah started the walk to her house just two blocks away, like everything else in Leigh Acres. She looked back and saw the pastor still looking her way and then awkwardly move his gaze as she turned. Hannah would have normally looked, even subconsciously, to see a ring, but hadn't, given the setting. She would have to come back another Sunday.

Hannah returned home to make her favorite: a triple-decker bologna on white bread sandwich. She never let any condiments or vegetables like tomato or lettuce take away from the purity of the sandwich. Afterwards, she spent the next two hours cutting the lawn before retreating to the front porch with an iced tea.

She found herself debating the minister versus the small businessman as potential mates and decided she was being foolish. Her musings were interrupted by sirens from the volunteer fire department rescue squad as it emerged from the corrugated building just a block away. Rather than departing out of town, it turned down her street and stopped just a few houses past Earl and Lisa. She walked over to their house to watch from a distance and see what might be happening. It was odd that her little world stopped at their house and she never really ventured to the other three houses beyond.

"What happened?" asked Hannah to Earl and Lisa, who now stood in their driveway.

"I'm guessing that Robbie Jones had another overdose," said Earl with a sigh. The rescue squad had arrived there once before for the same thing. A moment later, a gurney was rolled from the house with the teenager on oxygen to a waiting ambulance, which immediately sped off to the hospital.

"So the drug deals behind the cotton mill just moved somewhere else," said Hannah, shaking her head.

"Suppose so," concurred Earl.

Not far away, the strange little man was watching them both with an icy stare. *That boy was one of my best toadies before that woman started meddling at the cotton mill and he bought from somebody else. Now, I see her again.*

He walked the short way back to the obscure door to the building juxtaposed next to the mill. Overgrown branches covered the opening as if acting as a warning to stay away. The door croaked open and slammed shut. The foul stench of his work invaded his nostrils, but he just ignored it as he always had.

He chuckled as he looked at the bottle of "European Miracle Cure" on the old shelf. During prohibition, the next generation continued the family business by selling "rotgut" made once again by the mountain folk. But a few bad batches caused a couple people to lose their vision and a suspicious death. When people shied away from "shine," Grandad started buying legal denatured alcohol mixed with noxious chemicals to render it unfit for drinking and thereby allowed by prohibition. He learned to "wash" out the chemicals and resell the "miracle drug" with a heck of a kick.

Business took off and expanded beyond drunks to include local families who considered it socially acceptable and healthy to imbibe in "the cure." The skills Grandad learned were passed on to yet another generation, who learned to make more lethal drugs.

The little man became angry again thinking about how *that woman* was messing with a long line of elicit traditions, making his customers shy away with neatly trimmed mill grounds. But his anger seemed to be clouding his ability to think of a solution that wouldn't lead back to him and incarceration. He had to settle down. The answer was probably simple; he just hadn't thought of it yet.

Chapter 11
Night Action

At work the next day, Hannah processed a construction loan for a young couple. Her mind returned more than once to the drug overdose, but she shook off the image and focused on the business at hand. Often it broke her heart to have to say no to somebody who had so quickly destroyed their credit at the outset, but this couple had avoided any financial calamity in their young life. So, she was pleased to get an okay from the old scrooge in underwriting.

Since the couple was from Nitrate City, the closest branch for their appointment was actually in Leigh Acres. So, she was able to schedule a late-afternoon meeting there and exit the branch early to make for home. On seeing her, Baxter and Lilly scurried from the backyard through the cat door to the pantry containing treats for their pre-dinner snack.

With the cats' treats and dinner delivered without mishap, Hannah eyed the bucket of cucumbers and squash left by Lisa for dinner. Lisa was trying to introduce Hannah to anything healthy for the longest time and would be disappointed if they went to waste. However, the thought of cutting them and whatever else she had to do for preparation seemed monumental— especially since she really didn't know exactly what to do. Instead, she found the Spam lite and some instant pancake mix that required only the addition of water. Hannah paused and wondered, *If they invented instant water, what would you add to it?*

She reached in the lower cabinet and retrieved a dust-covered pan that originated in Girl Scouts, which was likely the last time she used it. After what felt like hand-to-hand combat with the batter and pan, which seemed to have become fused together, she extracted large wafers akin to cardboard. Hannah looked at her creation and decided it could be fixed with a triple quantity of syrup.

After cleaning up from dinner (throwing away the paper plate and washing the one lone pan), she sat down. She had contemplated just throwing out the pan and paper plate together but felt guilty. The cats took longer in their after-dinner cleanup routine, which carefully started with a licking of paws and ended with the face. Hannah marveled at how this same habit was probably executed by the breed for over three thousand years without change.

Hannah's smartphone rang with a call from Lisa. "What you doing?" There was no need to actually introduce herself. Hannah's only other callers were random wrong numbers, and Lisa knew it. The only people Hannah knew intimately were characters in books and every neighborhood animal, which she considered people.

"Just finished my dinner?" Hannah responded with a swallow.

"What did you think of the squash?" asked Lisa.

"It was good," lied Hannah.

"I knew you'd like it. You want some company? Or are you about to build a garage or something?" Lisa and Earl had a running joke about Hannah. Earl toiled each day in the sun or under some building. When he got home from work, he collapsed in a lawn chair. Hannah, on the other hand, was just starting up some home project or lawnmower, which drove Earl a little nuts. Earl cut his lawn once to every two or three times

Hannah cut hers. In truth, Hannah cut hers way too often, and Earl not enough.

"Where's Earl?" asked Hannah.

"Earl's off with his buddies at the marina," Lisa said with indifference. She and Earl seemed to have a comfortable relationship after years together. He liked what he liked, and she liked what she liked. They had reached a comfortable equilibrium.

"Come on over," said Hannah.

They sat on Hannah's porch watching a photographer and his subjects across the street. Lisa sat with her sweet iced tea and Hannah with her unsweet version. In the South, the quickest way to identify a Yankee was to see them drinking "unsweet."

"Taking pictures in front of a dilapidated old building seems strange to me," mused Hannah.

"Me too," agreed Lisa, "but at least this is a side benefit from all your lawn cutting."

As they sat, the local high school cheerleading squad began creating a pyramid in front of the cotton mill as a backdrop. They weren't the only ones. Photographers now sporadically appeared to take senior pictures, wedding pictures, and just about anything else in front of the mill. Apparently, it was chic.

"Lucky we aren't men like that man in sunglasses over there. Otherwise, we'd have to get a pair and pretend we aren't watching the girls too," said Hannah, pointing to the strange little man peering around the corner of a nearby building.

"That's just Mr. Hamady. His family owned the dry goods store. After he inherited it, he closed it up the same day. He didn't need the money, I guess. We see him time and again," said Lisa offhandedly.

They continued to watch as the pyramid got taller.

"If I tried to do what they're doing, I'd probably break a hip," complained Lisa.

"I don't think I could even get into one of those tiny outfits," added Hannah.

After a long silence, Hannah shared her findings about gang symbols at the library.

"That's good to know," affirmed Lisa. "Honestly, those symbols have been there for years, so 'snake' would probably be needing a hip replacement himself by now. It's the new spray-painted lines and random letters I can't figure out. At least they haven't returned."

"Since the markings don't match a normal teenager's musings, could they be something else, like a coven's calling sign?" asked Hannah.

"A coven? You mean like a group of witches and warlocks?" asked Lisa, now sitting up. "I think your imagination is running away. There hasn't been anything like that around here for years."

"So, there was something in the past?" asked Hannah.

"Yes, on the mountain. Those mountain folk are different with their superstitions. They don't do sacrifices or anything that I know of," said Lisa, sitting and staring as if thinking back in time.

"That's good. I'd hate to have to keep in my cats," said Hannah seriously.

"I really think the markings were just a mean-spirited joke to harass us for trying to spruce up the place," concluded Lisa.

The photographer and girls left, leaving Hannah and Lisa to other thoughts. After a while, Lisa went home to watch her favorite program. Not wanting to return to thoughts of covens and gangs, Hannah retrieved the journal, where Caleb and Ridge were comparing letters from home.

*****

"My paw says that he and some other federal minded men were invited to a meeting at Looney's Tavern. It was a fair distance on a corduroy road and he wasn't going to go at first, worrying that our horse would come up lame on the sideways logs. But he went after all. He said they signed some document that says Winston County has no quarrel with the Union and won't support either side of the war," read Caleb.

"My paw wasn't there, but said he heard about the document and finds it right smart. Everybody was talking about it and calling themselves the Republic of Winston," conferred Ridge.

About that time, other boys from neighboring northern counties converged on the two with similar letters.

"We best keep these letters hid," warned Ridge in undertones. "There's no sense raising the tempers of the other more Southern boys even more. We already have to watch our backs."

They whispered back and forth as a group debating what to do if the authorities came sooner rather than later and forced conscription into a Confederate Army.

"I'm for going home if that happens," agreed a couple.

"But how will we know they're coming before they get here? If we refuse, we'll be thrown in jail. If we go along with it and run off, we'll be shot as deserters."

"There's no sense panicking. Our families paid good money for us to be here. Maybe it will all blow over, maybe not. Either way, we need to break this up. We're drawing eyes on us," concluded Ridge.

They all went back to the respective areas in the barracks or off to other parts on the grounds. Caleb retreated to a log near the tree line. He was even more troubled than the others, given his close relationship with his grandfather and family correspondence with his far-away great uncle. As a kid, Caleb bragged that his seafaring great uncle had once befriended John Paul Jones, who confided the reason for his own escape to the American colonies.

Caleb stayed on the log until it was time to return to revile and bed. But when he got there, each cadet was packing a haversack.

"What's going on?"

"We're being ordered to a sham battle. We have to muster shortly."

"In the dark?" asked Caleb.

"Yep. The headmaster thinks that we should see the 'elephant' (battle) we're going to be facing soon enough and learn."

Caleb quickly stuffed a blanket and crackers into his haversack he had slung over his shoulder. A few moments later his squad was hoofing it a half mile through the woods with another quad. Two squads were marched into the opposite direction to act as the enemy. They barely got into place when the sweet sounds of crickets were replaced by cannon blasts and acrid smoke that filled Caleb's nostrils.

Caleb's squad was ordered to form a defensive line.

"You there, dig faster. The sham enemy is just yonder. You want to end up 'somebody's sweetheart' (dead soldier)?"

The cadet next to Caleb groaned under his breath, "How come the boys from southern counties are made voidettes and allowed to ride horses while we're forced to do the digging?"

"Just hush up," warned Caleb. "The cadet sergeant major is watching us."

The two sheepishly glanced his way as he called the squad leader Ridge to his side. After conferring, Ridge approached. "Half of you boys will be going into the woods to look for enemy patrols. Count off in ones and twos. The ones be ready to move out when I call."

Just five minutes later, Ridge called the ones, which included Caleb, to move out. Their orders were to move silently through the woods toward the enemy position. If they saw an enemy cadet, they were to call out that they saw them. By the rules of the sham battle, that meant they had to fall dead. The only ones allowed to carry guns were the squad leaders.

They made their way in the dark forest, keeping about ten yards from each other with the sound of cannons in the distance. As they made their way to the edge of a clearing and began to cross, they saw an enemy patrol on the other side.

"I see you!" was yelled by squad members on both sides simultaneously. Unfortunately, Bull was one of the cadets on the other side. He decided to settle the argument by forcing one of the smaller cadets to the ground when Ridge rushed forward to stop him. In the confusion, Ridge was hit in the head with the butt of a rifle. Caleb assumed one of Bull's toadies attacked Ridge from behind, but he couldn't tell for sure. Shoving and arguments among the cadets continued.

He kneeled next to his friend, now unconscious.

"Ridge. Ridge!" asked Caleb, but there was no response and blood on his scalp. "Stop your fighting now. We need help!"

It seemed to stop the scuffles and two more from Caleb's squad were limping and bleeding.

"You two boys run to get the cadet sergeant major. Tell him that we're dreadfully frightened that Ridge is hurt something fierce. We need one of the voidettes here with a horse to get Ridge back to the school."

Within moments the cadet sergeant major was there with another squad leader on two horses. They loaded Ridge onto a horse with a rider as best they could with two cadets on either side to walk the mount back to the school. The doctor wasn't due for another day so Caleb was sent ahead to fetch Miss Kate.

Ridge was brought into the infirmary affectionately known as Company Q, where Miss Kate applied cold compresses and sent another cadet to fetch some corn liquor from the quartermaster. Caleb went along and argued with Quartermaster Miller, who claimed he didn't have any because it was against school rules. When it was clear that Caleb wasn't leaving without it, he finally relented and remembered where he'd kept a bottle for "medicinal" purposes.

Miss Kate made Ridge drink a little and put him back to sleep. By this time, the two other cadets were brought in.

*****

Hannah's thoughts were cut short by a mournful cat cry, followed by the clang of the garbage lid nearby. The feline utterance came again, this time more shrill. Baxter or Lilly, she knew not which, was about to launch into a fight with another cat. Hannah jumped to her feet to avert the calamity that often resulted in a trip to the vet, or at the very least, tending a bad bite in the ear or other body part. Hannah rounded the corner to see a neighborhood tabby about twice Baxter's size. At the sight of Hannah, he ran. Unfortunately, that resulted in Baxter perceiving that his challenger was in retreat. So, he gave chase to collect his winnings in fur. Hannah followed but they disappeared in a nearby thicket, then she heard cat screams that accompanied a horrific fight. Hannah yelled Baxter's name again and again. They scuffled more, then Baxter tore through the bushes and retreated into the house cat door. Hannah chuckled as she thought of the Mike Tyson quote, "Everybody has a plan, until they get hit in the face."

It was late and she decided to leave the journal and prepare for bed. The concentration required to read the journal and decipher words left her exhausted. After feeding the cats, she retreated to her bedroom in the front of the house (next to the porch), where she turned off the light. She was about to fall asleep when a car slowed in front of her little cottage. Now having gone through three cuttings over the same number of weeks, the grass was beginning to look like a neatly maintained little park—certainly not suitable for a car to drive through to reach the back of the cotton mill to complete a drug transaction. The driver seemed to look her way and cuss, then drove off in a huff. A few minutes later, another car did the same. She realized that forcing their drug deals to a change in venue may be causing more animosity than she realized—even if not related to a gang. Tomorrow she would secure the house like only she knew from managing residential construction.

Back in the lab, the little man, Hamady, looked at his sunglasses. He had to be more careful watching potential recruits for that side of his business. Hopefully *that woman* thought he was lustily gawking at the cheerleaders for his own pleasure. But his pleasure was purely financial.

That little part of the family business was added by Great Grandad during the Civil War. He first heard of the profit potential when reading that Washington, DC., alone had more than 450 "public houses" catering to the troops. It was said that General Joseph Hooker and his men were such frequent visitors that the young women became known as "Hooker's Regiment" or simply "Hookers."

Just to the North, Nashville had more than 1,500 "public women" in an area called Smokey Row. The Confederate policy of confiscating food from local farms to feed the troops made local women readily available. They had to feed their children by any means possible, and Grandad was more than willing to supply the means.

Hamady himself knew that it was a dangerous business that could lead to discovery. But he was willing to take the risk. Besides, his high school toadies had no problem finding recruits now that Leigh Acres had again fallen on hard times.

The thought of toadies reminded him that with Robbie Jones's overdose, he had lost his best recruiter. Robbie was more than happy to be paid in drugs for each recruit until *that woman* started nosing around. Neighborhood gang symbols didn't convince her that the area was unsafe for a single woman. The answer was simple. The idea of "unsafe" had to be brought right to her front door.

Chapter 12
Sick Call

The next day, Hannah used her knowledge of home construction to crime-proof her home. She began by replacing the short screws in every outside door hinge and strike plate with three-inch versions. Hannah knew that short screws only penetrated the decorative door jamb surrounding the door that quickly splintered when kicked. The longer screws went well into the two-by-four frame that more than held its own against a swift kick. It wasn't guaranteed to stop a criminal, but it could cause them to break an ankle in the process.

With the doors reinforced, Hannah drove fake security signs in the lawn outside the front and back door typically associated with a monitoring service. Nobody would know the difference. Lastly, she borrowed an old trick that builders used to dissuade theft. She attached fake security cameras by the front and back door. They cost less than ten dollars and contained a simple battery that powered a motion sensor. When anyone approached, the camera moved back and forth as if watching their every move.

Satisfied, Hannah decided to check out the cotton mill. Maybe regular trips inside to build familiarity would further remove her anxiety after dark. If nothing else, she'd eliminate the possibility of cults due to the absence of charred wood with animal remains or new graffiti.

Hannah opened the creaking old door, now slightly askew due to a missing hinge. She pushed past the old rooms and looked at the old machinery, which stood dark and eerie in the barely lit center of the building. Light shone in, illuminating the rusty appendages that looked threatening, even in their inactive state. Hannah tried to envision people working to meet the demands of a growing war effort. She could only imagine the danger posed to workers, especially slaves forced to do the most dangerous work. There was almost a chill in the air as she wondered if any ghostly specter remained from a lost life. Hannah tried to adjust her eyes to the darkened space that looked like a poorly taken photograph in black-and-white.

The sounds of a passing motorist downtown seemed to create a ghostly moan that made Hannah shudder once again and think about the danger posed by being alone in an area that may have any number of structural deficiencies. She turned and tripped over an old bottle, sending her to the floor. She laid there waiting to feel the first pangs of pain from an injury but found none. But from this position, a small shoe caught under the machinery captured her gaze. She reached for it at full length and managed to tear it from the machine's grasp. Hannah took this find outside to examine it in the light. It was an old-style Victorian ankle boot, obviously from a child.

Hannah knew that children in the industrial revolution worked in factories twelve to fourteen hours a day. They were often used to dislodge items that temporarily jammed in large equipment by crawling under or even into machines. The factory owners justified their lack of decent wages and poor working conditions as providing the orphans with food, shelter, and clothing. The fact that the children were often maimed or killed didn't enter into the argument.

Hannah went home and cleaned the shoe. She then placed it on a shelf. It was a sad reminder that there was actually a little life with hopes, dreams, and fears attached to it. She wondered if that little life survived to adulthood. Either way, she kept it almost as a family keepsake of a lost loved one since she had none of her own. Maybe that was why she was so intent on reading the journal and finding out what had happened to the cadets.

Hannah glanced out the window and saw Lisa. She had obviously come home from work and decided to check on her friend.

"Too bad some kids had a field day with a few rocks," commented Lisa, looking at the new collection of broken windows across the street. With the grass cut, even kids felt free to approach the mill with impunity.

"Yes. Never have so few been owed a spanking by so many," said Hannah, chuckling at her own joke. Only a history geek would have recognized the parody of the Winston Churchill quote during the Battle of Britain, referring to the heroic work of firefighters saving London from ruin, saying, "Never in the history of mankind has so much been owed by so many to so few."

"How about you? Any floating apparitions?" asked Lisa with a fake smile meant to hide a serious question.

"Well, not floating," answered Hannah with an equally contrived seriousness.

"I'm not kidding— are you okay?" asked Lisa with the smile now gone.

"Yes. I've rounded the corner but feel fine," said Hannah proudly.

"That's great. Now let's turn to something more fun. I know you're hesitant to go down the dating hole, but anyone interesting on the horizon, like a vendor for the credit union?"

"No," said Hannah emphatically without any hint of "fun."

"Nobody at all?" pressed Lisa. "You know that if I don't get any information, I'll be forced to bring back my friend from the football game."

Hannah looked at her, waiting for her to say, "just kidding," but nothing followed.

"Well, I went to the Presbyterian Church and thought the minister was intriguing, but for all I know he's got a wife and twelve kids."

"The minister, huh?" said Lisa, now contemplating the match. "Why was he so intriguing?"

"He mentioned that he was also some administrator at the university."

"He mentioned that in his sermon?"

"No, just to me."

Lisa straightened up, indicating that this was getting interesting. "I need details, details. Spill it, sister."

Hannah described their brief interaction at the front of the church. Then, Lisa said, "I know old Muriel at that church. She'll know his story."

"No way," announced Hannah emphatically. "A question about the availability of the minister to one of the people at the church will set the grapevine on fire. Forget it."

Lisa looked disappointed but agreed, secretly thinking she could figure out how to get the information another way. With that, Lisa left with the excuse of going to watch her favorite TV show. Hannah knew otherwise.

It was only five o'clock, so Hannah retrieved a beverage from the kitchen, triggering two cats flying into the room yelling "Yow!" at the pantry door. After chastising, but giving treats to the two, Hannah decided she needed a brief road trip out of the house. The day was pleasant, so she chose a leisurely drive to the ruins with a blanket, bologna sandwich, and chips in tow.

After the short ascent up the hill, she parked and approached the entrance. The gate to the central grassy area was closed, but there was plenty of room to walk through gaps in the white decorative fence. She found a spot under a tree near the walled ruins and began to eat and read.

*****

Caleb returned to Company Q to check on Ridge. There he found the doctor giving Ridge a spoonful of a mixture that made him gag.

"Why you treating a cut by having him drink something? Shouldn't you be applying some herbs in a cool rag to the cut? That's what my grandma learned me back home," observed Caleb.

"You see this, young man?" the doctor asked, pointing to a medical certificate emblazoned with "Certificate of Surgery."

"Yes, sir, but..."

"I don't care what they did in that bug hill you came from. You need to leave doctoring to your betters." The doctor then left in a huff, presumably to complain to the headmaster.

Caleb ignored the comment and stayed by Ridge, who promptly threw up. "You look awful puny, Ridge."

"I was feeling better until that doctor showed up. He took off the herb mixture that Miss Kate had put on my head and kicked her out."

They spoke for a few moments more before the headmaster entered with the doctor.

"Master Rochester. May I see you a moment outside?"

Caleb didn't bother answering and quietly followed the headmaster in defeat.

"The doctor says you've been disrespectful."

"I just asked why he was treating Ridge's head with something he put in his stomach. It seemed like Miss

Kate had things well in hand before he got there," answered Caleb.

"Miss Kate is a fine woman. But she ain't a medical school-educated doctor with a certificate to prove it. Now you run along," said the headmaster firmly.

Caleb angrily marched off, muttering to himself without paying any real attention to where he was going. As he rounded a corner, he ran headlong into Millie, knocking her to the ground.

"I'm so sorry, Miss Millie," stammered Caleb as he reached down to help her up.

"I'm all right," she responded, brushing off her deeply faded dress that showed more than its share of wear. They then stood in an awkward silence.

"I'm sorry if I got you in trouble with your paw. Truth is, I was happier than a lark when we was in the kitchen together and didn't think about us being unchaperoned."

"He was awful mad," admitted Millie.

"My maw sent me some lasses and jam. Maybe we could share it sometime."

"I don't know. My paw would skin me alive."

"He wouldn't have to know. We could meet on Sunday a while after services at the chapel. It's respectable and quiet. And besides, the cadets will be released from chores for the Lord's Day and skedaddle."

"I reckon so. What would we have with it? You can't eat molasses and jam without something to put it on," said Millie.

"I don't know. That's all my maw sent," lamented Caleb.

"I know. I'll ask Miss Kate if we can have some leftover pone," said Millie, bright-eyed.

"The idea's worth a goober, all right. I'll meet you there," exclaimed Caleb.

With that they both left before Millie got in trouble for talking to a cadet. Caleb had a whole new outlook.

*****

The light was beginning to fade, so Hannah closed the book. Before grabbing her blanket, she took a brief walk around the ruins to see if she could discern the location of Company Q. Unfortunately, that wooden shack was long gone along with the others. But she could envision with a smile the two young lovers bumping into each other and the scene unfolding. She thought, *The answer's so simple. I just need to get me some pone and lasses for my man.* The only thing missing was a good man. Maybe one would appear on the way home.

Chapter 13
Another Try at Love

The next day, Hannah left work and contemplated her next stop. The university library was an option, but her hunger and thought of junk food won out. So, minutes later, Hannah found herself in front of a freezer case for her all-time favorite, a Tombstone sausage and pepperoni pizza. That in hand, all she needed for culinary perfection was a small Jimmy Dean's sausage roll to break up and sprinkle on top before baking. Most people didn't know the secret of cooking a Tombstone pizza. It's in the crust. Namely, place the pizza directly on the oven rack (no cookie sheet or pizza stone). It comes out a crunchy and golden brown.

Hannah's small business owner was behind the counter.

"You hurt your head?" he said with a look of concern. Hannah almost forgot that she had clipped a jagged two-by-four while examining some framing and had to put on a Band-Aid to stop the bleeding. In the absence of a Band-Aid, she was known to use super glue or duct tape for similar injuries gathered in some home improvement project—just to keep working. Unfortunately, she knew that her medical skills rivaled her cooking prowess.

"It was just a minor accident."

"It doesn't look minor. Do you need some medicine? I don't have much, but I carry some aspirin and antibiotic ointment."

"Okay," agreed Hannah.

Shallow 107

"Besides, you should always have some around the house for the husband and kids," he said somewhat clumsily and waited for her comment back.

"No husband or kids. Just me and two cats. And, I think I'd come out with more cuts and bruises if I tried to apply antibiotic ointment on them."

"Me either. A wife, I mean. I have a daughter that stays with my ex. I have to wait until every other weekend to get her."

"That's nice," commented Hannah. "I'm sure she looks forward to your time together."

As usual, the store suddenly had three people behind her. She was probably being paranoid, but she could have sworn the two teenagers who suddenly appeared were snickering at the old coots trying to get a date. So, she just smiled, said goodbye, and left.

Returning home, Hannah felt that something was missing. Then she realized that the porch light was broken and the camera gone. She looked around and saw broken glass on the floor and the camera next to it where it had fallen and broken open, revealing the batteries. She thought, *How strange! I could have sworn that I screwed that in really well. If it was only the camera that had fallen, I'd assume I attached it to soft wood. But with the light broken, it means that somebody has been here.*

She felt angry and decided to walk over to the mill. She didn't know what she was looking for but hoped her feeling of vulnerability would be decreased by seeing that the two things weren't connected. After a brief walk inside, she tripped and dropped her soda can from the gas station between a machine and the wall in an area too difficult to retrieve—so she left it. There was obviously nothing here to worry about. The vandalism must have been high school kids walking through the neighborhood on their way home. Nothing she couldn't handle.

Returning home, Hannah pushed the incident from her mind.

Not far away, Hamady retrieved the soda can that Hannah had dropped. He thought, *It's bad enough that everyone from photographers to kids now approach the mill. Now she's venturing deep inside. Surely a single woman would have concluded that the neighborhood is unsafe and move after viewing the new gang symbols and having her home vandalized. It's so simple. Once she's gone the grass will grow tall again, the mill will become an eyesore, and people will stay away. Then my customers can return for their midnight purchases. Why hasn't a "For Sale" sign appeared in front of the house? I'll give it a couple days.*

Chapter 14
Grandfather's Musings

The next day, Hannah was called into the office of her boss, Clyde Higgins. It seemed that he had gotten a call from another contractor who had complained that this little girl was poking around his projects too much.

"So, why did you call him anyway?"

"I noticed that we had done a draw on two lot takedowns and didn't see their locations noted anywhere. In fact, I couldn't find the files at all, and just wanted to know where they were," she said defensively.

"Well. They aren't assigned to you, so don't worry about it."

"But all new residential construction loans are to be inspected by me. It's my job."

Old Higgins was starting to get mad and then seemed to compose himself. He straightened his bow tie adorning his blue and white striped seersucker suit that screamed his gentile roots. It was slightly out of place in time and seemed to clash with his slightly orange hair due to excessive doses of Grecian Formula. "He's an old friend of the family and I take care of his projects."

Hannah was silent for a moment. Then subtly pressed a little more, saying, "Just for my education, where are they? Is it an area that I can help you with on route from one of my other visits in the same area?"

"That's very gracious of you, but I can handle it. You have to let an old man get his exercise," Higgins said with an artificial grin.

They sat in silence across the desk from each other until it became conspicuously long. Then, Hannah said, "Okay, then." She stood and Higgins said nothing more. So, she left the room thinking, *This could be job ending for one of us. Unfortunately, I know which one.*

She drove home almost in a daze. She thought about talking to Lisa, then rejected the idea. It was probably nothing and he was completely sincere. It wasn't the first time she'd had to stay out of the crosshairs of a highly connected good ol' boy. So, she decided to dismiss the idea, feed the cats, and enjoy her leftover pizza. To get her mind off her fears, she opened the journal once again. But her mood went from bad to worse.

*****

Ridge and the other cadets had now been in the infirmary for the better part of a week and seemed to go from bad to worse. Caleb noted, "It was as if the very hand of heaven's again him." Company Q seemed to be turning into a "mare's nest and there's scarce room for hope." He asked the doctor what was wrong and was told that they had "ague."

*****

Hannah was puzzled and looked up "ague." It seemed to refer to a severe mystery flu that was treated with anything from quinine to carbonate of iron. Unfortunately, this flu was only a mystery because the primitive medical practitioners of the time had no idea what the ailment really was, which ranged from malaria to hepatitis. One apparently more-popular doctor treated ague with a drink plied with opium. The scariest treatment involved ingesting a spider web every two hours until the ague subsided, or presumably, the patient died, whichever came first. Hannah returned to the journal and the story began again.

*****

Miss Kate hung blue glass bottles in the trees around the school. Caleb asked her why and she said, "Evil spirits can't cross water and are afraid of the color blue. When you have a blue bottle, they can't help but go inside. In the morning when they see its blue, they get scared and can't think how to get out. I check the bottles every morning. When I see something that looks like a moth or other such bug, I knows it's really a spirit in disguise and so I cork it. Then I throw it in the river so nobody can get at it and let it out."

Miss Kate went on to say that she had asked the headmaster to paint the infirmary blue to keep the spirits out. But he refused, saying she was just being foolish and that God was their protector. Instead, he put healing oil on the head of each cadet with a special blessing.

She explained with self-satisfaction, "The headmaster did allow me to hang a mirror next to the front door of the infirmary. So that's almost as good."

"What does a mirror do?" asked Caleb.

"That old Sam Hill, the devil, can't help but admire hisself in the mirror and stays there all night until the morning sun chases him away."

"What does the doctor say about the mirror and such?" asked a dubious Caleb.

"That doctor don't hold with it, but won't say anything since the headmaster said it's okay."

"I had not entertained the notion to do these things for Ridge, but I ought to have. Up to now, I always did what my paw learned me. I hold my breath when passing a cemetery so I don't get possessed by no spirit coming up my nostrils. And, I'm going to go straight away and overturn one of Ridge's shoes to ward off death," announced Caleb as he turned to rush off.

Miss Kate and Ridge left like two people on a mission to do doctoring the right way. Later that night, Caleb tossed and turned in anticipation of his Sunday meeting with Millie. The next day, hours passed after the church service with no Millie. Depressed, Caleb sat in the empty chapel. He tried reading the Bible for comfort, but there was none to be found today.

The next morning, Caleb stood in formation and listened to names being called. They newly arrived cavalry officers read off names, upon which the cadets left their ranks and made their way to the waiting men.

"It's a great honor to be granted a commission in the cavalry. It is a testament to the families of these men that arranged for such a posting. In the coming days, the rest of you men will be likewise summoned to protect the Southern way of life."

With that said, the formation was dismissed and the young men surrounding the cadets expressed their congratulations. Those already granted exemptions, including Bull, expressed their regret at having to remain home for the greater good, claiming that if it were up to them, they'd be right there in the fight to come.

The boys from the northern counties faded to the back. With Ridge still in the infirmary, Caleb had emerged as the unofficial leader despite his junior cadet status.

"At least them boys will be in the cavalry. They have a better chance of not becoming somebody's sweetheart dead on the ground in the infantry where we're headed," came the complaint.

"I wish Bull were going," said another. "But at least some poor horse has been saved the agony of carrying that lump of lard to the front." That brought a subdued chuckle from the group.

Caleb said nothing. He knew that they all would have to join, be conscripted, or refuse to fight in the coming days. If they joined or agreed to be conscripted, it meant betraying their families who supported the federals. If they refused to fight, it meant being branded a coward in jail. There seemed no right answer as "shame opposed the best notions of my thought."

Caleb told the squad to "skedaddle before we cause a ruckus" and walked off. He knew he had to make a choice soon. He sat on a log and thought of his grandfather and home. He recalled one of his grandfather's most cherished memories of the Revolutionary War as it drew to a conclusion. His unit of Continental regulars marched to North Carolina to engage with the enemy in the battle of Guilford's Court House. His grandfather had bragged about it being known as the "the largest and most hotly contested action in the South." The Americans lost the battle, but Grandfather and his fellow soldiers took pride in that they weakened the larger British force, so much so that Cornwallis moved to Yorktown for reinforcements. There, he was defeated by George Washington and the French fleet. Caleb's grandfather described the story so often that Caleb had it memorized.

It was late, as his grandfather gazed at the clouds moving along the remaining treetops. Unfortunately, many of the trees lay strewn about like sticks reaching in all directions. Some had fallen prey to cannonballs. Others were chopped down by battlefield engineers attempting to build defensive earthworks. His grandfather's gaze moved to the men beside him. Like him, they were ragged from head to toe. Some had pants ripped to the knees and no shoes. Most were almost skin and bone from months of deprivation.

He himself, had a few adornments on his simple blue jacket. Unlike the day it was given, it was now faded from battles and long hours of work in the forest. In dramatic contrast were the French soldiers standing opposite the Americans, with their brightly colored blue, white and yellow uniforms. They stood gleaming against the fading sun. Many looked at the ragtag American troops with contempt. French soldiers and sailors alike saw the Colonials as amateurs who would surely have been defeated if it weren't for the French naval guns that kept the British fleet away.

But his grandfather didn't care. He looked upon them with equal contempt. He wondered how many would have joined the army to go without pay, food, clothing and shelter as the Americans had. Looking at the French soldiers with their plumes waving in the wind, he guessed that most would have just stayed home. How many had endured or seen what he'd seen?

In the distance, drummers could be heard beating the cadence for the marching soldiers in their slow advance on the Americans. Within moments, he heard the stomp of seven thousand British infantrymen striking the beaten ground as they marched in unison. He saw British General O'Hara, a subordinate of Cornwallis leading the column. Caleb's grandfather was later told that O'Hara stood in for his commander who feigned sickness rather than face the shame of defeat.

Like the French, the British soldiers had bright, ornate uniforms signifying a professional European army. When his grandfather had previously seen them in battle, they were behind flags with bright battle streamers. Today, however, the flags were encased in canvas covers as a sign of shame in surrender. As O'Hara arrived at the American line, he dismounted to present his sword to Washington, who likewise now stood on the ground.

Washington, characteristically, waived the honor. Instead, he directed O'Hara to surrender to his subordinate. Some British soldiers were stone faced; others openly wept as they surrendered their weapons and slowly walked back to Yorktown, now prisoners of the Colonials. General Washington politely directed that the sword just given be delivered back to Cornwallis.

Caleb recounted the event like he had been there himself. He took great pride in his grandfather's role in creating a new nation. This pride was countered with bitterness at talk of the Union being simply a "legal compact" that could be annulled if the states didn't like its policies.

In addition to his anguish over prospective conscription, Millie had gotten word to Caleb that she was a virtual prisoner in her paw's cabin. He had caught her with the "pone" sneaking out to meet Caleb that Sunday. Putting two and two together, he made her stay in the house under fear of a beating.

*****

Hannah paused to contemplate the gravity of the situation. She had to remind herself that it happened over a century ago.

It was still a nice night, and she decided to change her mood by enjoying the present. So, she retreated to the hammock strung between two trees in the backyard out of sight of the cotton mill. Baxter and Lillie followed, and she soon had a feline lying on each leg. Their purring seemed to keep it all in perspective and make danger seem a lifetime away.

Just fifty yards away, Hamady was contemplating what to do with *that woman* as he worked away in the mixing room. Anyone entering would see working tables stained with chemicals and a little blood.

Bordering the tables was sporadic modern equipment. A hum could be heard from machines efficiently performing their tasks.

Hamady reached toward the shelf containing the old family elixir. But instead of the antique bottle, he grabbed a blank pharmaceutical container next to it. When his father had inherited the business hidden in the backroom of the now-closed family store, he had branched off to something new.

He found that fake antibiotics were the easiest to counterfeit because patients didn't expect any immediate effect. The problem was that his father was too soft-hearted. He didn't see the true potential of illicit drugs—or the price people would pay for subtle poison to eliminate that pesky spouse. The more Hamady thought about it, the more he wondered: Why not use this skill to send Hannah a message if no realty sign appeared soon on her property?

Chapter 15
The Riddle

Hannah survived the next workday, and on Saturday she arose and found Lilly and Baxter waiting for breakfast. After feeding them, she decided that the weather was too nice to start any work project and sat on her front porch sipping iced tea. She thought about life back in Chicago, where this kind of quiet was impossible. So, she pushed out feelings of guilt for being unproductive and sat a while longer watching the birds eat from her feeder while squirrels darted out occasionally to steal any seeds dropped on the grass. After a while, she tried to raise herself out of the chair by force of will, but gave up. Her mind wandered back to Caleb and the school, where she knew the walls seemed to be closing in on the young cadet. So she retrieved the journal from the living room and started the story once again.

*****

Caleb had come to the realization that there was only one way out. He had to save Ridge, Molly, and himself in the only way possible.

Ridge was in the infirmary getting worse instead of better. The doctor was either incompetent or had a vendetta against Ridge because of being labelled a federal sympathizer by the cadets from southern Alabama counties. So, it was likely that Ridge would never leave Company Q a living man. If Caleb did nothing, Ridge might shortly be in the cemetery.

Millie was likewise a prisoner in her own home. Her paw wouldn't let anybody near her for fear of "sparking" (dating). Caleb was convinced that if he could get Molly back to Winston, his mother and father would welcome his prospective bride with open arms. In his heart, Caleb noted that he knew she might be just running away, but he didn't care. He was in love.

Caleb began to "have notions of deliverance enter my mind to make some escape by taking Millie for an elopement and finding liberty for Ridge." He planned to fetch Millie in the dark of night right under her father's nose. Then with the help of Millie, "our next care will be to fetch Ridge off the academy's grounds." The task of retrieving Ridge had taken on new risk now that Bull had taken up residence in the infirmary a day earlier. Bull's father had directed that since he was now an apothecary in training, he deserved a more appropriate lodging for his professional status.

On top of that, Caleb wrote, "Once we gain our liberty, we can't divert ourselves to hunt for food due to Ridge's delicate condition, so we need to be gettin' supplies from the supply shed." Among other things, they needed blankets and food for the slow trip with many stops for Ridge's recuperation.

The plan had to be completed now or never. All they had to do was survive being caught by Bull in the infirmary, stuck with the quartermaster's Arkansas toothpick in the supply shed, or being made Millie's dead sweetheart by her father.

Hannah was now flying through the journal with unbridled anticipation when Lisa and Earl came up.

"We decided it was too nice a day to work and thought we'd visit our favorite Yankee," said Lisa.

"Can I see the journal that we've talked so much about?" asked Earl, pointing to the journal in Hannah's hand. She handed it over while Earl was careful to keep her place.

Lisa and Hannah lazily traded comments about the birds and the weather when Earl handed the journal back. "Funny how it ends with a poem."

"What do you mean?" asked Hannah.

"See," said Earl, pointing to where Hannah had stopped.

The next entry was a rhyme in a different script. She had been interrupted in her reading just before seeing it. And, Earl was right. There was a riddle in what appeared to be a different handwriting, or maybe just a different pen.

Then, the pages after that were from another cadet entirely. Paper was obviously scarce and the cadet was probably happy to find a partially unused notebook. Hannah looked at the journal almost in a panic and read aloud.

> *Like Paul who fled from murder a deed he did, to meet a man who unlocked a heaven's light hid,*
> *But enemies would follow him ashore, as a crown pursued a good man the more,*
> *So, Caleb and Ridge did the same, to reach an end with poor Richard's name.*
> *One will be buried in blue and the other in view.*
> *While a Shakespearean sonnet this is not, Venture to the Tempest to find the spot.*

"So, what does that mean?" asked Lisa.

"I don't know," said Hannah. She then relayed the recent entries since they had last talked.

"So, we don't know if Caleb wrote it to taunt his pursuers? Or, another cadet wrote it to describe the ending fate of Caleb and Ridge?" observed Earl.

Reading it again, Hannah said nervously, "It seems more like something to be placed on a tombstone. Like the way somebody died."

They sat for a minute and Earl announced, "Well, we can't let it end like this. We have to figure it out."

"How?" asked Hannah, now pouting.

"We ask the descendants which one killed him."

Lisa tried to calm the situation. "Let's just start with analyzing the riddle some more. We have to figure out who Paul is."

They all read the riddle again.

"Is Paul somebody who's fleeing a murder, who then killed Caleb?" asked Earl.

"I don't think so," said Hannah. "It says 'like Paul.' I think it's referring to another situation. Or, some historical literary reference."

"Maybe Millie's father killed him when he tried to take her home? Or, maybe he got in a fight with the quartermaster when he went to steal supplies for their journey? Maybe Bull or the doctor did it when he came for Ridge? Maybe the other cadets got him?" interjected Lisa. The theories came so fast and furious that Hannah and Earl just looked at her with an expression like *you're not really helping here*.

They sat for a moment while Hannah read it yet again. "I'm not sure he was killed; he may be the one who killed somebody." She recited the first phrase again: "'Like Paul who fled from murder a deed he did.' Then, it says, 'One will be buried in blue, and the other in view.' Does that mean buried right after this writing or much later?"

"Is Paul a cadet?" asked Lisa. I don't remember you mentioning anybody by that name."

"I didn't," said Hannah.

They discussed the riddle back and forth and all the suspects for another hour. They still weren't sure if Caleb and Ridge died or did the killing. But they all agreed that they had a murder. And, it all involved Caleb and the people at the school. The only question was, could they ever solve it?

Chapter 16
The Debate

After work the next day, Hannah went to see Bert at the library. She thought maybe other school records might make reference to Caleb, Ridge, or Millie. If so, that could easily close their little mystery. If not, maybe they could find a reference to Paul from the riddle. Bert helped Hannah find a few additional documents within another box, but no journals. She took the additional records with names, supplies, and log entries of comings and goings, but she knew it would take tedious scrutiny to find any reference that might be irrelevant anyway. She dejectedly walked across the abandoned lot to her little house.

After feeding the cats, Hannah sat sulking on the porch.

"You look like you lost your best friend," said Earl from his truck, shaking Hannah from her preoccupation.

Hannah rose and went to the truck. "Not my best friend, but I feel like I lost a couple friends from the school."

"I know it. Lisa and I talked about it until well into the evening. We'll all get together and talk about it in a little while," said Earl, putting his truck in gear.

"Okay. Keep your stick on the ice," said Hannah absentmindedly. Earl paused with a look of confusion, so Hannah added, "It's a reference to hockey. Don't get a penalty for 'high sticking.' It's an expression from the 'true north' (Canadian border and higher) to mean 'stay out of trouble.'"

Later, Hannah, Lisa, and Earl sat in the driveway petting Houdini and Sugar Ray, who seemed in need of attention. Hannah wondered if Baxter and Lilly, who had wandered twenty-five yards away watching, were jealous, then turned back to Earl and Lisa.

"I know I'm a little obsessed with the journal. Maybe I should just let it go," commented Hannah.

"No more than us," observed Earl. "I made Lisa give me an update on your reading every night and I've been pondering about Caleb and the others. I especially want to know about what happened to Millie. Did she run off with Caleb? Or just stay with her father and be forced to marry Bull, whose pap could give her a dowry?"

"And besides," said Lisa, "what if they did come to a nefarious end? They could have gotten lynched by any number of those others. My point is, they deserve justice. It's like Caleb wanted you to find that journal. They need to be laid to rest properly."

"Do you think it's a coincidence that you found the journal?" asked Earl.

Hannah paused to see if he was teasing Lisa about some netherworld attempt at communication. But the look on Earl's face indicated he was "dead" serious.

"I don't know," said Hannah. "Who knows God's plan for anything? Maybe something good could come from it. And, then again, maybe not."

"What do you mean, maybe not?" asked Lisa.

"She means," interjected Earl, "asking questions to their descendants about their feelings against the war or implying that maybe their grandpappy was a medical quack or a crooked supply man will cause friction."

They all mused on the pitfalls.

"Well, I think you two should go for it," commented Lisa.

Hannah looked at her again to see if this was a joke, like *go ahead and charge; I'll be right behind you.*

"I mean it," Lisa continued. "I think we all agree that we can't solve the riddle without getting more information. Earl knows everybody in town and their kin. You know how to research books. Earl can ask around to figure out who might know something and you can interview them; take Earl along."

They all thought about it for a few moments while enjoying the summer breeze and numerous fireflies.

"So, if I'm Freddie and she's Thelma, which one are you? Scooby-Doo?" asked Earl finally.

"I'm Daphne, the pretty one," smiled Lisa with satisfaction. "But Freddy is too much of a 'dande' (pretty boy). You're Shaggy and you know it."

"Well, at least I'm not the dog. That's you, Houdini," said Earl, scratching the dog's stomach. Houdini responded with his characteristic tail wag that seemed to overtake his whole body.

"I guess we'll just have to tread as lightly as possible. Maybe it's easier to start with determining if Caleb and Ridge were alive when they left the school. They either went home or were conscripted into the Army," said Hannah. "Unfortunately, tomorrow is Saturday. So, I can't make any records requests from archives until Monday."

"In the meantime, EJ can help us," said Earl. "He knows the Civil War buffs locally. They know just about everybody who served. They might already know what's in the records. Let's just shake the tree and see what falls out."

Hannah thought, *But what if an axe falls out, on our head?*

In the nearby building, Hamady leaned over the lab table making one of his lethal formulas. In a strange way, he took pride in his work. He told his select clients that poisoning lacked the crudeness of a knife or bullet and had an elegance all its own. He had his favorite ingredients based on the specific request. Strychnine was at the top of the list because of its rapid absorption and dramatic effects that put on quite a show. Cyanide was almost equally impressive, followed by so many others, including digitalis and even morphine. He had his least favorites too. He didn't think much of arsenic. It was passé and went all the way back to the Borgias.

No. Today he was using his favorite: belladonna. It had a royal quality, having been used by the Emperor Augustus to eliminate family threats. He thought, *There couldn't be a more appropriate way to protect the family business.* Then, he had another thought: *Poisoning that woman so close to the lab will bring too much scrutiny from the police.* After a few more minutes, it occurred to him: *Killing one of her tiny family members wouldn't draw any attention at all. I'll just have to bide my time and wait for the right moment. Then, she'll get the message and be out of here as fast as a scolded cat.*

Chapter 17
Sons of the Confederacy

It was Saturday. Hannah crawled out of bed and went to the kitchen, followed by two cats. They were perturbed that she slept in and hadn't given them their breakfast. After opening a can of gourmet cat food, Hannah grabbed herself an iced tea and made toast. The cats were initially confused as she lingered in the kitchen using the toaster that they had only seen once before. This was the closest thing they had witnessed that approached actual cooking since she microwaved canned chili. Besides, there might be something for them. Determining that it wasn't, they continued with their breakfast while Hannah brought her toasted creation to the front porch.

Earl pulled his truck in front and called Hannah over.

"I talked to EJ last night but didn't mention our quest," he said. "He asked me for help moving some stuff out of an old shed at LaGrange. Do you want to tag along? I thought you could explain what we're looking for. But be careful. He might not react well to the thought that some cadet wasn't supportive of the cause."

Hannah looked at her toast and said, "Let me grab some jeans. Be right with you."

After a quick change where Hannah slipped on jeans and a beach T-shirt with "Gulf Shores Alabama" printed on the front, they were on their way to the ruins.

"So, any thoughts about how we broach the subject of Caleb and Ridge joining or fleeing?" asked Hannah.

"EJ may not take too kindly to that thought. Most folks around here have an idealized memory of the war with all southern boys being likeminded. I think we should approach that topic carefully," cautioned Earl.

They talked about a way of broaching the subject for the rest of the ride and soon arrived at the ruins. The two set in to work with EJ, dragging old farm implements from the shed before taking a break in three chairs with the old man.

"So, Hannah," observed EJ, "how's that old journal? Still reading it?"

Hannah and Earl traded glances before Hannah answered cautiously, "Yes, EJ. In fact, I've become enthralled with a couple of the cadets named Caleb and Ridge right before the War of Northern Aggression. Some of the cadets were raring for enlistment."

"I suppose so. Our southern boys knew where their loyalties lied," confirmed EJ. This wasn't going as Hannah might have hoped.

"That's just it, EJ. Some of the boys were from northern Alabama counties that had no plantations. They seemed to be less inclined to enlist in the army than the boys nearer Montgomery."

EJ contemplated her comment, sensing that there was more to it. "So, what's the issue?"

"I'm trying to figure out what happened to some of those boys. Was there any talk that some of the cadets chose not to enlist?"

"Who maybe helped in some other way," added Earl, trying to avoid confronting EJ's idealistic image of the boys all marching off tighter for the cause.

"No. I ain't never heard that kind of talk," said EJ, sounding irritated with wide eyes.

Earl tried to tread even lighter. "Was there some unit you know of that Hannah could look up to see if they joined together?"

EJ pondered the question. "I know that many of the boys left to join up, and the few remaining cadets when the school closed went into the 35th Alabama Infantry Regiment. But, I believe there weren't enough to form a company. I suppose they were all split up to spread the young officers among various companies."

"Okay," said Hannah. "That's a start."

"But I know who might know more. You should talk to Ernie White. He's the local chapter president of the Sons of the Confederacy. If anybody knows about what happened to the boys, he will. In fact, they're having their monthly meeting tomorrow afternoon in Mushoals. I'll call him. He's always looking for a speaker. Can you whip up your Native Americans in the Civil War talk?" Hannah had mentioned at the reenactment that she had once spoken to a history group about Native American participation in the Civil War.

"I'd be glad to," confirmed Hannah.

EJ walked a short distance into a small building that served as their office and welcome center. There, he looked up his friend's number and made a call on a landline. A couple minutes later, he emerged with the address and said that he hadn't had a speaker at a meeting for several months and jumped at the chance. After a little more lite conversation, Earl and Hannah left. She retreated home to find an old PowerPoint of her talk.

The next afternoon, Hannah went to the Muscle Shoals Library for the meeting. It was closed. After walking around the building, she found a side door that led to a meeting room with two folding tables at the front for the members, totaling less than a dozen. In the folding chairs making up the gallery were another half dozen family members. Given the age of the men, Hannah assumed that the family members were mostly designated drivers for an elderly parent.

Hannah grabbed a folding chair in the makeshift gallery next to a daughter knitting to pass the time. After reviewing the meeting minutes regarding who owed for the coffee fund, Hannah was introduced as the speaker. They seemed surprised that she was formerly in the Bureau of Indian Affairs. Hannah presumed that female speakers in the past covered genealogy and more social topics. She handed out copies of her PowerPoint, which seemed to impress the members unaccustomed to overly prepared talks. She then launched into her description of the role of Native Americans in the Civil War.

"Most people don't think about the role of Native Americans in the Civil War. Just as the war pitted brother against brother in the white world, it did the same within and between tribes. Colonel Stand Watie, a chief of the Cherokee Nation, called all males between eighteen and fifty into Confederate military service. Watie quickly became seen as a genius of guerrilla warfare and the most successful field commander in the Western Mississippi."

Hannah went on to describe various Native American units and battles in different theaters of the war. "In Oklahoma, much of the Creek and Delaware tribes sided with the Union despite being relocated from their homes in the East."

She couldn't help but focus on her own tribe. "Are you familiar with phrase 'war eagle?'"

"Of course!" replied a few enthusiastic Auburn fans. In response, the University of Alabama fans answered with a defiant "Roll Tide." Hannah knew that while the tiger was the official Auburn mascot, most students and alumni identified with the school's traditional motto and fight song that featured 'war eagle.'

"You can thank my own Lac Du Flambeau Chippewa tribe as the probable source. Back in 1861, Chief Sky retrieved two baby eaglets from a tree and gifted one to a man named Dan McCann. McCann raised the majestic bird and ultimately presented it to the 8th Wisconsin Regiment in the Civil War. The company renamed their mascot 'Old Abe' and adopted 'war eagle' as their battle cry. After the war, the now famous bird became a resident of the Wisconsin Capital Building before returning to Dan McCann to live out his days in peace." After several minutes of excited discussion among the Auburn fans, Hannah concluded her remarks with, "At the close of the war, General Ely S. Parker, a member of the Seneca tribe, created the articles of surrender signed by Lee and Grant at Appomattox Court House on April 9, 1865."

Following polite applause, the meeting moved to normal business and concluded with an invitation for any new business. There, Hannah interjected, "I was hoping to ask members for any thoughts on where the cadets at LaGrange Military Academy went on to serve in the Confederacy." A couple members described their ancestor's role and their army unit, but none of their family members had attended the school. So, they didn't know anything about what happened to the 35th Alabama Infantry. The evening turned out to be a bust.

"Do you have any thoughts on who might know more?" asked Hannah politely, trying not to show her disappointment.

After the meeting, a daughter said, "You could try the University of North Alabama (UNA) library. I believe they have a few references to local families that had members who served."

Hannah thanked her. It wasn't much of a lead, but it was something. It also provided a perfect excuse to see the handsome library administrator—even though the interval since their last meeting was too short to make it seem unrelated. But that couldn't be helped.

Hannah crossed the little campus from the oversized parking lot to see a world populated entirely by teenagers intent on looking older than their age. They seemed to move with slow progress, mostly in packs of three or more. Many wore cutoff shorts and sweat clothes that Hannah wouldn't even have worn in the privacy of her own home on laundry night. She felt older than her age and definitely "uncool" or whatever term they used today.

Hannah entered the library and was reissued another visitor pass after noting her area of research for today on the form. The student behind the counter had offered to fetch the library administrator, given Hannah's unusual area of study. So much the better.

"Well, hello again," said the Reverend Mike.

"Hello," said a self-conscious Hannah. She didn't want him to think she was stalking him at work.

"Robbie informs me that you need to examine some war records," he said, smiling.

Rather than give the whole story, Hannah just said, "I was reading that parts of North Alabama were not necessarily in favor of secession and I was attempting to research certain cadets at LaGrange Military Academy who had served in the Confederate Army or went back home."

"Your comment about North Alabama seems correct," confirmed Mike. "I looked at the voting records at the time of secession for another project.

Since slaves in these counties comprised less than one percent of the population, they had less impetus to support the war from a strictly economic basis, if not moral. So, their voting delegates were generally in favor of staying in the Union. They saw no reason to leave the country over guaranteeing slaves as free labor for plantations, of which they had none. After spirited debate, only two-thirds of the delegates voted for secession. One delegate in particular from Winston County refused to sign the final document to secede from the Union and was arrested."

"That's where my cadets hail from," affirmed Hannah.

"Unfortunately, I don't have detailed records of Confederate unit rosters. For that, you have to go to the Montgomery Archives. I do have some general information on the founding families of Winston County. But, for more on individual records like birth, death, and land ownership on your cadet, you have to actually go to the county records office in Winston County, I'm afraid. I can get you addresses for both."

"That would be great. In the meantime, I'll look at any references to the founding of Winston County," said Hannah.

Just then, Mike was summoned by another student library worker for a phone call, which Hannah detected was the object of some disappointment, and directed the original student where to find the records for her. She sat at a table with various documents and found that Winston County founding families included the Bells, Stocktons, Tittles, and Ingles. So, Caleb's family was not among them. Other references indicated that President Andrew Jackson's father hailed from the county. And, after Jackson's presidency, many of his political followers settled in the county. Andrew Jackson was an ardent defender of the Union, versus states' rights, in addition to being linked with common people against wealthy interests. To that end, he vetoed the continuation of the central bank, which he said was "prostration of our government to the advancement of the few at the expense of the many." When South Carolina prohibited the enforcement of federal tariffs, he obtained the authority to send troops to South Carolina to enforce federal laws. South Carolina subsequently backed down and Jackson preserved the Union in its greatest moment of crisis to date.

So, Hannah concluded that Caleb's grandfather probably came to the county after Andrew Jackson's presidency. He was probably among the families, like that of Ridge, who followed Jackson politically. As a result, they were pro-preservation of the Union and politically in line with the rights of commoners versus wealthier interests. That corroborated the journal and gave Hannah confidence that the rest was authentic, and the riddle or epitaph sincere.

As far as the county went, the influx of Jackson followers may have contributed to the area having over six hundred families without slaves and only fourteen with slave ownership, most of whom belonged to only two households. One local historian concluded that the residents of Winston County were born to Union families and attended Union schools with Union beliefs.

"Did you find what you're looking for?" asked a student worker.

"I think so. Tell me, do many people examine these records from around the Civil War?"

"I think you're the first since I've been here. Some people do research on the founder of UNA. Since the man who founded LaGrange College was the same that founded UNA, they tend to do research on

LaGrange as an afterthought. Apparently, he was quite the racist."

"Wasn't everybody back in those days?" said Hannah slightly defensively. "He was a man of his time."

"I guess it went beyond that. He wrote some controversial stuff about slavery being ordained in the Bible—pretty off the wall," said the student casually while he began refiling the research.

"That is pretty off the wall," confirmed Hannah. "I'll have to come back to research that. Thanks for the tip." Hannah's education was grounded in a Christian University and she was no stranger to the Bible or biblical commentaries. She thought that slavery was universally condemned by most clergy—even in the past.

"Dr. Mike asked me to give you these addresses for the county and state archives. He also asked me to apologize for not coming back himself. He was called to the dean's office."

Hannah thanked him again and made her way out of the library in a line of students looking fatigued. So, Mike had a PhD but didn't use the title. That was a plus.

Looking at the students, Hannah could see books under their arms ranging from chemistry to accounting. She shuddered and thought to herself, *The next time I miss the good old days, I need to come here and see the textbooks to bring back memories of calculus: the scourge of my existence.* As she walked further, she thought about the student's reference to the headmaster of LaGrange Military Academy. Maybe the quartermaster wasn't the only one up to some shenanigans. It appears that under the headmaster's ministerial robes sat a man much more conflicted than she realized. Maybe even in the clinical sense. She had to find out more.

Chapter 18
Montgomery

A day later, Hannah approached the old municipal building in Montgomery. Crumbling mortar showed great gaps between pre-Civil War bricks. It seemed perfect in keeping with the rundown neighborhood in which it stood. Uncut grass stood before sporadic houses and storefronts now left to ruin, half of which were boarded over. An old African-American man was sitting on a bench and seemed to read her mind.

"This was a great neighborhood back when I was a kid. Coming here was like Christmas. We'd look in the store windows and dream. Now, it seems like everybody moved to the suburbs or buy their trinkets on the internet rather than visiting a store."

"It's too bad," added Hannah. "I think we've lost our sense of community, and maybe a little bit of our link to the past. I know future generations will probably condemn us for the mess we've made. And rightly so."

"Are you one of those Civil War buffs? It seems like they're the only ones who come here."

"Sort of," said Hannah, now sitting next to the old man. "I'm actually trying to figure out what happened to a couple young men who were against the war."

"That would make you the first, I reckon. Everyone else just wants to look up their family soldier claiming they fought to preserve the South," he said with some disgust. "I'm not sure what was worth preserving about one man owning another."

"I agree. And truly, it appears that a lot of Alabamians felt the same way, primarily from northern counties. Up there, the families worked their own land and didn't own slaves."

"So, you're trying to find out more about a couple of those men?" he asked now with some interest.

"Yes."

"My granddaughter works in the records room. Maybe she can help. I'll tag along if you don't mind."

"Sure thing. I'd be glad to have the help," said Hannah, a little relieved. She was dreading going into some old government office and asking for records without having the proper forms.

Hannah and the old man went inside and down an old hall that led to a room with an old piece of wood over the doorway that read "Records Room." Inside, a woman in her twenties looked up and saw the two standing together. "Granddad, are you two together?"

"Yep, I've come to help this young miss find somebody," he nodded.

She smiled and said, "Any friend of my granddad is a friend of mine. Who are you looking for?"

Luckily, the office seemed to be devoid of any other requesters, so Hannah felt free to explain about LaGrange Academy and the journal. They both listened intently until she was done, then looked through Confederate records for the names Caleb Rochester and Ridge Bailey—focusing on the 35th Alabama Infantry Regiment. They found nothing.

"Sorry," apologized the granddaughter. "Maybe they died at the school or were never conscripted into the army."

"I guess not," said a dejected Hannah.

"Let me do some additional research into a couple other possibilities and get back to you," she offered.

"Yes, we'll get back to you" added her grandfather.

This drew a warm smile from both women.

Hannah returned home to find Lillie meowing frantically at the car door. She sensed that something was wrong and followed her to find Baxter shaking and throwing up next to a food bowl on the porch. The problem was, their own bowls were inside in the laundry room. The food was obviously tainted.

In a panic, she called Earl and Lisa and asked where to take him. Earl said he'd be there to pick her up in two minutes. True to form, Earl was there in his truck in a flash and waving for her to get in with Baxter. She jumped in the passenger seat.

"Doc Miller is at a farm just up the county road tending to a horse. His wife is calling him to be ready," said Earl while screeching the tires.

Minutes later they were skidding to a halt on gravel in front of a barn. The vet and the farmer were standing by. The doctor grabbed Baxter and quickly made a determination: "This cat's been poisoned."

He reached in his bag and gave the feline an injection. Within seconds, Baxter stopped his convulsions and seemed to breathe normally.

Hannah couldn't speak, tears running down her face.

"This little fellow will be okay, miss," said the doctor. "You got him here just in time. You can hold him."

All Hannah could do was whisper, "Thank you."

Chapter 19
Paul

Baxter laid in Hannah's lap on the front porch, where she refused to let him out of her sight. Lisa and Earl sat on either side in total confusion. They had just started their inquiry. How could anybody be mad already?

"Could it be a cult?" asked Hannah. "You said that they had strange superstitions in the mountains. Could it be that I've been poking around LaGrange too close to their doorstep?"

"I don't think so," responded Lisa. Then, after a slight pause, she added, "Sacrificing a cat would certainly fit a witch, and we did find an old five-pointed star painted on the mill behind the grass. Could it have been a territorial marker of some coven?"

They discussed the point a little further, with Hannah pointing out that some Native Americans like her father believed in witch-like spirits walking the earth called *Yee Nahgloshi* or Skin Walkers. After dismissing the thought as folklore, they decided that the poisoning was a hateful prank. Hanna wasn't entirely confident about that conclusion but knew for sure that Baxter and Lillie would become inside cats for a while.

With that settled for now, they took stock in where they stood in the investigation. All the while, they watched a couple take what appeared to be engagement pictures in front of the mill. They were in the area they had just painted to cover the graffiti as one of their backdrops.

"That's nice to see," said Hannah with Lisa and Earl nodding in agreement.

They then took stock in where they were in their little mystery.

"So, the Confederate records didn't turn up our cadets. That leads back to the riddle and our other suspects. Have you had any revelations about the riddle?" asked Earl.

"Not really. I've been doing research and all I can think of are Bible references to the Apostle Paul. That makes sense given our location in the Bible Belt and the timeframe." Hannah repeated the riddle out loud.

> *Like Paul who fled from murder a deed he did, to meet a man who unlocked a heaven's light hid,*
>
> *But enemies would follow him ashore, as a crown pursued a good man the more,*
>
> *So, Caleb and Ridge did the same, to reach an end with poor Richard's name.*
>
> *One will be buried in blue and the other in view.*
>
> *While a Shakespearean sonnet this is not, Venture to the Tempest to find the spot.*

Hannah continued, "Prior to his conversion to Christianity, Paul was dedicated to persecuting the disciples of Jesus Christ. In fact, the Book of Acts indicates that Paul took an active part in the martyrdom of Stephen. So, that would correspond to the riddle's reference to 'Paul, who fled from a murder he did.'"

"Wow," said Earl, "I had no idea he was such a bad guy."

"Well, he was initially, but he acknowledged that upon his conversion. Prior to becoming a follower of Jesus Christ, Paul was a leading rabbi who saw the early Christian Church as leading Jews astray into believing that Jesus was God. Paul saw his efforts to wipe out Christians as necessary to protect the Jewish faith. But, Paul later repented and recognized his sin. In fact, in the Book of Acts, Paul says he persecuted the Church 'beyond measure.' But that was the point; who better to witness to the fact that Jesus was God than the most prominent opponent? Given that he was also a murderer and the acknowledged greatest persecutor of the Church, it also showed that no matter what the sin, anyone could be redeemed. Jesus' death on the cross paid for his sins.

"The only problem with the riddle is that Paul didn't flee from the murders. He was arrested and transported to Rome. So, it could just be the way it's worded, but that could be an issue," continued Hannah.

"Well, the rest still ties into Paul," said Lisa, continuing to quote the riddle, "'a man who unlocked a heaven's light hid' refers to Jesus, right?"

"Possibly," continued Hannah, "if you interpret 'unlock' as meaning that Jesus unlocked the secret to Heaven or Jesus as the Messiah. But a theologian would argue that it was no secret. Jesus taught over and over that he was the Lord incarnate and sent to earth to show the way to heaven."

"It could just be a difference in interpretation between you and Caleb. Everyone knows that there's no shortage of denominations due to these differences," said Earl.

"You're right, Earl. Paul seems to be the likely man referenced in the riddle."

"So, what about the next part? "'But enemies would follow him ashore, as a crown pursued a good man the more.' That part seems to fit the Apostle Paul," reinforced Lisa.

"It's true. After his arrest by his enemies, Paul was shipwrecked on the way to his trial in Rome by the emperor. But he wasn't exactly pursued by his enemies at this point. He was already under arrest. Unless the reference is to another shore."

"It could be that, or you're just overanalyzing," commented Earl. "Paul still seems to be the person being referenced on multiple levels. And, he was going to be tried by the emperor himself. That's certainly got to be a reference to the crown."

"I suppose so," agreed Hannah. "But what about the next sentence, 'So, Caleb did the same, to reach an end with poor Richard's name?' It's true that Paul was killed a martyr in Rome. That would make it clear that Caleb, Ridge, and possibly Hannah were martyred for supporting the North. But then who's Richard? And, while we're at it, why did they use the phrase *'with poor Richard's name'* instead of *'in poor Richard's name'*?"

"Could Richard be another cadet in the school who was also murdered?" asked Lisa.

"I just don't know," admitted Hannah.

"And what about the Shakespeare reference? My Shakespeare is a little rusty. Otherwise, I'd have that cracked," chuckled Earl as if it was a language all its own, which it was in a manner of speaking.

They discussed the riddle for another half hour, and all indications seemed to point to some involvement with the Apostle Paul. They didn't have any clue as to the Shakespearean reference other than the fact that it was a mysterious play. They decided to leave it entirely for now and focus on determining what happened. But, they certainly needed more information, and it could only come from LaGrange Military Academy and its descendants. With that conclusion and the approaching dusk, Earl and Lisa departed for home. Looking at the mill, Hannah couldn't shake a feeling of foreboding. The old building might look like a chic photo opportunity in the daylight, but nighttime was another story. She brought the cats inside and locked the doors.

Earl went to work the next day calling friends and relatives to find any local descendants. Earl struck out on the doctor but found that James Miller, the quartermaster, had a great-grandson still living locally. The quartermaster's descendent occupied a prominent position as head of the Seed Association. He likewise found a descendent of the dry goods store owner who supplied the school.

Earl couldn't find a direct descendent of the reverend headmaster but did locate a great-grandniece. Earl's contact also thought the local First Methodist Church might have some records or older members from the mountain who might know something.

That left Millie's father. There seemed to be no descendants from Millie. She truly seemed to have fallen off the face of the earth. But a local farm family existed that appeared to be a descendent from another child after Millie.

Doctor Fosburgh had a descendent but nobody seemed to know where she went after getting married. They said she was always a bit "off" and suspected that any information obtained might be faulty.

A quick look at Winston County's white pages didn't show any Rochester or Bailey. And, none of Earl's friends had any connections that far away. In truth, it was only half an hour, but that's a world away in rural Alabama, or any other state for that matter. That research would take more work. The big question was: where to start?

Chapter 20
The Doctor

The next day, Hamady casually walked by Hannah's house and saw both cats in the window. He thought for sure that his favorite poison mixture in the cat food would have done the trick. Obviously, he didn't anticipate the cat's keen sense of smell. It probably just got a whiff of the poison and turned its nose up at the food rather than eating it, which saved its life. Nevertheless, *that woman* had to be afraid of the neighborhood now. He had every reason to believe a realty sign would soon appear. If not, he'd have to make his message black-and-white.

Hanna sat at the Leigh Acres Library table combing through the doctor's medical log she'd returned. Baxter's poisoning reminded Hannah of an observation Caleb had made in the journal. He noted that he had challenged the doctor's use of a mystery medicine on Ridge that coincided with his physical deterioration. She studied the sick log but didn't see any deaths recorded that could implicate him in killing Ridge or other patients. But in truth, she really didn't know what she was looking for. However, she did find what looked like a certificate from a medical school. Thinking that the doctor may have other patient records somewhere with their deaths recorded, she spent an hour researching him on the library's computer. She didn't find anything, but in the process, located a library in Huntsville that carried old records from the medical school he attended. Hannah decided that the best place to start was meeting with the man she found to be the caretaker of the old school's records. Maybe he could provide information on the doctor and knew of some other records repository. He was also far removed from Leigh Acres and unlikely to be offended by questions regarding the doctor or his training. So, to Huntsville she went.

Hannah got out of her car and made her way to the old building, where a library volunteer brought her to Dr. Robert Green. He was an older man, slightly hunched, with gray-white hair wrapping around his bald head. As he approached, you could almost hear his joints creaking in protest. But as he got closer, his bright eyes and smile seemed to reduce his age by decades. He stood as a reminder that, while life has stopped giving and begun the slow process of taking away, you can still be thankful for each new day and the knowledge it brings.

Hannah extended her hand. "I'm Hannah and I was hoping to tap your brain for a moment if you have the time."

"I'm old, so leisure is something I have in abundance to share, but time may ultimately prove more elusive."

Hannah had to pause to process the statement and attempted a clever retort. "Well, I'll consider you chronologically gifted instead of old, but I'll still be sparing with your gifts."

The old doctor laughed and said, "Fair enough."

"Are you an MD? Or another type of doctor?" asked Hannah to determine the right questions to ask.

"I'm a doctor of pharmacy. I taught at the University of Alabama at Huntsville. I'm now retired and have an interest in Victorian medicine. After considerable research here, I found that I knew the records better than anyone. So, they asked me to become a library volunteer managing this section. It actually works well for both the library and myself. Folks like yourself come in with questions that generally pique my interest. In your case, I didn't find the name Fosburgh in the school graduation records for any of those years."

"That's puzzling," said Hannah. "I saw his name on a diploma for surgery from the school."

"The school diploma wouldn't have said anything about surgery. That would have been an attendance certificate for a specific lecture."

"The students earned diplomas for specific lectures?" asked Hannah with obvious confusion.

"Not diplomas," countered the old man, "just certificates that looked very ornate. Here, let me show you."

The two walked to another cabinet, where he withdrew a certificate from a student's file. It looked just like a diploma with ornate lettering and their name written in an elegant script.

"This looks like what I saw," said Hannah.

"That explains the confusion. You see, most students never finished the entire course of study to become a physician. They bought a ticket to a lecture and received one of these certificates proving their attendance."

"So, for the surgery certificate, they just witnessed a surgical procedure on a person, or cadaver," said an incredulous Hannah.

"It was worse than that," chuckled the old man. "In those days, practicing on dead bodies was against the law. The student would have watched a physician explain it with the use of a blackboard."

"So," continued Hannah, "Dr. Fosburgh, or should I say Mr. Fosburgh, only attended a lecture and passed off the certificate as a medical degree?"

"It appears that way," said the old man. "But, that wasn't entirely unusual. At the time of the Civil War, most so-called doctors for both the Union and Confederacy never graduated from medical school. That's part of the reason they simply amputated limbs for injuries that would be considered relatively minor today."

"What about medicine? How did they know what to prescribe for disease and other illnesses?"

"They really didn't. In the bigger cities like Boston and New York, there were pharmacists known as apothecaries, and medical doctors. In reality, they were all pretty much the same at that time. Both dispensed drugs after diagnosing patients. Both prepared drugs from home remedies or recipes, which was their version of prescriptions. They made their remedies from anything: ground-up shells, flower pedals, you name it. Out in the rural South, things were much worse. Almost everything from measles to typhoid was treated with coffee...or whiskey. About the only ingredient that we would recognize as a medicine was quinine. Some clearly lethal chemicals like mercury were also given for any ailment. And, let's not forget bloodletting."

"It sounds like the last thing you wanted to do when sick was go to the doctor," concluded Hannah with a shudder.

"It gets even more morose. At the time of the Civil War, most physicians never attended even a single lecture at a medical school. They learned the trade as a brief apprentice with another doctor or even a family member who helped friends with folk remedies. The only positive was that chloroform was in use. At least most patients were asleep during their treatment, normally an amputation."

"How did they learn to administer chloroform?"

"They used the drop method in a cloth. When the patient fell asleep, they operated," the old man said with a shrug.

"What happened if they woke up?" asked Hannah with a shudder.

"If they woke up, they woke up. I suppose it was better than the percent that died from over-applied anesthetic. Did you know that a capable surgeon in the war could amputate a limb every ten minutes?" said the old man with some minor excitement.

"I'm not sure that's an enviable accomplishment," answered Hannah.

"After a battle, many worked all night. Plus, lack of water meant they didn't wash their hands or medical instruments, which were typically limited to saws and hammers."

"It sounds like doctors had the same tools as a carpenter," observed Hannah.

"That's pretty much the case. In fact, at sea during this time, a ship's carpenter generally doubled as the ship's surgeon. In a strange piece of trivia, Arthur Conan Doyle, the creator of Sherlock Holmes, was ship's doctor *and* the resident harpooner on a whaling ship."

"So, you're telling me that solving mysteries and medicine have always gone together," said Hannah, trying to make sense of the last piece of information.

"No," said the old man, "I'm saying that if you let me talk, we'll be here all day. Why don't you tell me what you know about the LaGrange doctor instead?"

"Well, I don't know virtually anything about him. But there may have been some student deaths." Hannah described how some students went into the infirmary for physical injuries from night maneuvers and got continually worse under his care.

The old man reflected for a moment. "They were young and should have had some chance of survival despite bad doctoring. It's possible that the doctor was experimenting with his own cure."

"What do you mean?"

"Some doctors fancied themselves medical researchers and created concoctions with everything from poisonous herbs to cow's urine."

Hannah was silent. Was she witnessing another Josef Mengele, who conducted experiments on prisoners in Nazi concentration camps?

"Do you really think he was experimenting?" asked Hannah

"It's possible; many did. There was so little medical knowledge, they tried various home remedies on many of their patients. So, experimenting wasn't done on a mass scale. It may have been done with the best of intentions, especially in a small school. But more than a few deaths would have raised the eyebrows of the locals—even with the death rates in those days."

"If he did experiment, could he have continued during the war without being as easily noticed?" asked Hannah.

The old man paused for a moment. "I suppose so. There were actually more deaths in the war from disease and poor camp hygiene than from actual injury. He could test his home brews with less chance of being noticed."

"Do you know of any place he might have kept records on his patients? How do I research a physician's war record?"

"There's no place for his records that I know of. If he was a Union doctor, you could make a request from the national archives. But being from Alabama, I'm not rightly sure," said the old man with obvious disappointment at not having every answer. "Let me call an old friend of mine in Montgomery. He has a medical exhibit he brings to Civil War reenactments. Maybe he might know of some local records."

After conveying her appreciation, Hannah departed for Leigh Acres. Every question seemed to lead to other questions. Even if the doctor was experimenting on cadets or Confederate soldiers, being released from the Confederate Army would hardly be proof. She had to think.

Driving home, Hannah's phone rang. She didn't bother looking at the number; it was either Lisa or Earl. Which one specifically didn't really matter?

"Hey, buddy," she said with a slight snicker.

"Hey, Hannah. I checked around and found something on that doctor's descendent for you," said Earl with some background noise that sounded like a circular saw. He was obviously working late on a job site.

"Great. But is this a good time?" asked Hannah, not wanting Earl to lose a limb.

"It's fine. I needed a break. It's going to be a long night. The dentist that's going to rent this old building is coming in to see our progress in the morning. We're trying to finish up some trim before then. You know how things look much farther along with some paint and trim covering up the rough edges. Anyway, I was talking to a friend of my cousin. He's a HVAC contractor and it turns out that his grandmother was kin to a patient of the doctor. Anyway, he had me call her niece, who's a genealogy buff tracking her family back to the 1700s. She figured out where his great-grandniece is. It turns out she got married and moved not far from Leigh Acres. I got her phone number and address for you. She lives in Cherokee, about thirty miles up Highway 20."

"Good work, Earl. By the way, how you holding up?" Hannah often worried about Earl. The kind of work he did takes a toll on the human body—especially after so many years. In this case, trim work meant a lot of kneeling and bending in tight spaces. A dental office would have a lot of little rooms with no shortage of corners. It would wreak havoc on Earl's joints.

"That's why I'm taking a break. I'm on the floor with my legs stretched out. I want to take off my boots but I'm afraid I'll never get them back on. It won't be more than a couple more hours. Then I'll get home," said Earl flatly, the spring in his generally happy-go-lucky voice gone. Hannah could almost sense a feeling of foreboding from her friend.

"Hang in there. Who knows, maybe we'll find something interesting and write a book about all this," said Hannah, trying to introduce levity.

"Yeah," countered Earl, "that will be the day."

Chapter 21
The Doctor's Secret

Dust seemed to be blowing around Hannah's feet as she walked on the dirt path leading to the large house. Hannah could see a few lights lit in the stately home. It was bordering on poor manners to visit after 7:00 p.m., but Hannah was slow getting out of work and had called in advance. The call itself was strange and seemed to fit the woman's reputation perfectly. She was evasive but agreed to Hannah's request all the same when she found that it related to her interest in genealogy.

Hannah climbed the porch steps and reached the door, knocking three times. At first there was no sound. She almost turned around and walked away, taking it as a bad omen. Then, she could make out the faint sounds of footsteps in the back of the house. Strangely, the light emanating from the windows was almost gone as the resident extinguished lights as she went. Adding to the strangeness, Hannah realized that the footsteps weren't far at all. The walker, whoever it was, had removed their shoes to make less noise. Only the sound of the creaking floor gave their position away, directly opposite Hannah on the other side of the door. But still there was silence as if the person was waiting for something.

Hannah had a feeling of dread and quickly decided to leave. This same scene must have played out in hundreds of horror movies over the years. Each time, the person went inside. Hannah quickly turned to leave when the door bolt loudly slammed and the door creaked open just a crack.

"What do you want?"

"I'm Hannah Sparrow. I'm here to see Ms. Cochran. We spoke on the phone."

"Is it just you?" the older woman asked, looking around the street. Hannah hesitated, thinking, *If I say yes, are you going to produce a syringe, stab me in the neck, and incarcerate me in the basement, making me dress as your late husband?* Her hesitation went on too long.

Finally, Hannah admitted, "I'm alone."

Now the silence from the other side was deafening and equally uncomfortable as the other person obviously debated what action to take. Especially given Hannah's long hesitation before answering that may have indicated some covert plot on her part.

Hannah added, "If another time would be more convenient...?"

"No, no," came the reply. "Now is convenient."

The door finally opened halfway. Hannah could barely make out the form of the woman in the shadows. She wasn't large and Hannah thought she could take her in a struggle, assuming she didn't have the syringe handy.

"Come in, come in. I'll give us some light."

Hannah cautiously entered the darkness of the room, partially shielding her head in case of a blow. Hannah could make out her figure walking along the back wall to an adjoining room to light a gas lamp.

She couldn't help herself and asked, "Does the house have electricity?"

The great-grandniece responded, "I'm not partial to electricity. I do things the old way."

"Then how do you conduct your genealogy research?" Hannah asked, not guarding her thoughts at all.

"The computer," she answered crisply.

Hannah stared at her and she seemed to sense the incongruity, adding, "It's an old computer."

With the flick of her wrist, there was light from the gas lamp and Hannah could see her. She was almost elderly and well dressed, even though on closer examination, the clothes seemed to be worn from a century of use. The dress was dark gray with about a thousand buttons down the front. Noticing her stare, she asked, "What do you think of my dress?"

"I like it," lied Hannah. "But I have to warn you: my friends call me 'Hannah—not a slave to fashion—Sparrow.'"

She laughed and Hannah's anxiety level dropped. She was certainly eclectic, but probably not dangerous.

"I've always been stuck in the past," she said smiling. "I'm also getting forgetful and just awoke from dozing off before your visit."

"I'm stuck in the past myself. As I mentioned on the phone, I'm researching some old journals from LaGrange Military Academy and I ran across someone who appears to be an old ancestor of yours," said Hannah, peering from left to right, trying to determine where they'd go next. They stood in a long, wide central hall with doors on each side. In the old days, it would have been a called a dog trot that separated two sides of the home, splitting the center. It served as a breezeway through the center to cool the family in the hot southern summer. Hannah assumed it received its name from having dogs cooling themselves that weren't allowed in the house itself. Today, both ends were closed off with front and back doors.

"Since we're talking about family, let us adjourn to the drawing room." On the way, they stopped at a butler's pantry where she had a pitcher of sweet tea. "I'm afraid it's turned to 'Yankee ice' (a drink with little or no ice, as if they came from a northerly climate where people presumably consumed little ice)." Hannah just smiled, thanked her for the drink, and followed to the drawing room.

Hannah was enough of a history buff to know that the drawing room was equivalent to today's family room. It was so named because the family "withdrew" from visiting guests to have private time.

They sat in two chairs on either side of what appeared to be an old game table.

"So, tell me what you've found," she said.

Hannah described the school and her cadet. However, she initially left off the part about her inability to verify any physician training or having some prejudice against the cadets from a poor farming and the possibility that he may have been experimenting on cadets.

"I do have a couple questions, though," said Hannah with some trepidation. "First, where did he get his medical training?"

"The Medical College of Huntsville," she said breezily.

"I saw his certificate, but it appears to be for a lecture and he's not on the graduation roles," said Hannah timidly.

"What are you implying?" she said with a steely stare.

"I'm not really implying anything," said Hannah, uncomfortably adjusting in her seat. "I understand that a lot of doctors elected not to complete the entire course of study and focused on the courses they needed. I was wondering if that was the case here. Or, if he went to school elsewhere." In truth, she thought the man attended one lecture for an hour to receive the certificate to pass himself off as a doctor.

"He went to the Medical College of Huntsville," she said again. "Their records are obviously spotty from years of mismanagement. Or, they were destroyed by Sherman's men during his march to the sea."

She was perceptively lying. So, Hannah decided to move to different questions.

"How about medicine? Do you know what sort of things he prescribed?"

"I'm sure whatever he received from the local apothecary. I understand they were very good in those days," she said with equal indignation.

Hannah inwardly chuckled to herself. As somebody lost in the past, the great-grandniece had to know that doctors fulfilled both roles and made their own medicine. She likewise had to know that the medicines were far from "good" at that time.

"Did he go on to serve as a surgeon for the Confederacy?" asked Hannah with a forced smile.

"He did. He served right to the end of the war."

"Do you have an interesting anecdote from his time in the service, or know the unit?"

"I don't," she said with an equally fake smile. It was obvious that she was done.

"Well," said Hannah after an uncomfortable pause. "I've taken enough of your time. Please don't get up. I can show myself out." It was obvious that she wasn't getting up anyway.

As Hannah closed the front door, she thought, *There's obviously something strange about this so-called doctor. I'll have to expand my research to any war records and anything else I can find. Earl found this lady, maybe he can dig up scuttlebutt about her past also. I'm sure the apple didn't fall far from the tree.*

When Hannah got home, she realized that she had forgotten to retrieve the mail in several days. She found the usual junk mail, along with a blank envelope obviously left there by a passing motorist. Inside was a note written in an almost childlike handwriting that read, "Put things back to how you found them and mind your own business or move. Otherwise, you'll be sorry."

Hannah stared at the note. The whole situation was like Alfred Hitchcock's formula for most of his movie plots. A regular person in the film kept thinking that the danger or intrigue they were suddenly pulled into wasn't real and must be their imagination. Then, something happened that made them realize they were in serious danger. In this case, this was a real threat. She was shaken and called Earl and Lisa over in a panicked voice. Earl arrived first at a full run with a baseball bat. "What's happened? You sounded shaken on the phone. Is somebody here?"

Lisa arrived seconds later. Hannah just handed over the note, trying not to cry. They read it aloud.

"Are you okay?" asked Lisa, putting her arm around Hannah.

"Yes, I guess so," she said shakily.

Earl took the note and read it again. "It's odd how they say 'put things back to how you found them.' That doesn't make sense."

Hannah agreed. "If our investigation is causing people to become scared or uncomfortable, you'd think it would say simply to 'stop.' It's not like we can put the genie back in the bottle."

Lisa took the letter back. "Well, I hate to say it about my neighbors, but maybe it's just a case of bad writing.

We're overanalyzing somebody that just doesn't express themselves well."

They were silent for a minute as Earl retrieved iced teas from the kitchen, trying to show they weren't going anywhere. Neither Baxter nor Lilly begged for a treat, despite Earl's proximity to the pantry, sensing that something was wrong.

After they all moved to sit, Earl concluded, "I really think it's just a cranky old neighbor who doesn't like change—especially from a Yankee. They're certainly not dangerous. The note doesn't mention violence. It just says that you'll be sorry. That could mean anything. Like, you'll be blackballed if you ever try to join the Rotary Club."

"I guess you're probably right," said Hannah with relief.

"And, besides…we're here twenty-four-seven, and there's a group of us doing this, not just you. People around here know who we are. They'll know it's all of us they have to contend with—including Earl's friends. We'd garner enough votes to get you into the Rotary," said Lisa with a chuckle.

Hannah smiled at the thought. Earl was connected to everybody in town, and they all had his back.

After further reinforcement, they calmed Hannah's nerves and agreed to proceed with the plan. With that decided, Earl and Lisa went home. Despite the cavalier attitude he projected to Hannah, Earl kept a wary eye on Hannah's house at all times.

Chapter 22
The Headmaster

The next day, the three reconvened for beverages on Hannah's porch to catch up. Since they had dismissed the note, Hannah moved on to describe her interview with the doctor's descendent in detail.

"She's obviously ticked off and hiding something," concluded Earl.

"Yes, I agree," said Hannah. "She probably knows that he wasn't a real doctor. But, that wouldn't have caused her to shut down like that. Most of the Civil War doctors weren't degreed. There's something more."

"The fact that he probably made his own medicine wouldn't cause her to lie either. That was also common. So, I don't think that's it either," reinforced Earl.

They paused for a minute, watching a couple getting their photos taken for what appeared to be their engagement. What made it interesting was their constant disagreements about some pose or another.

"Maybe they should take this as an omen," commented Hannah.

"I know, right?" said Earl. "He needs to learn the secret words used by husbands in any marital situation. 'You're right, I'm wrong, I'm sorry.'"

"Good boy," said Lisa, who was sitting next to him.

"Speaking of love," said Hannah. "Do you think that there was more to the relationship between the reverend and Miss Kate than master and slave?"

"I suppose so," said Earl. "But he had a lot to lose if it became public."

"I'm not sure," countered Lisa. "Half African, half white children of the slaves who looked like the master were common in the South. People just ignored the obvious as a social convention."

"But those were situations where the master basically raped the slave. Which, oddly enough, was socially accepted to a degree. A loving relationship would have been unthinkable," countered Earl.

"How tragic," said Hannah, stating the heartfelt obvious. "It should have been the other way around."

"So," concluded Lisa, "even if he did love Miss Kate, their relationship would have to be kept secret at all costs."

"But that's hard to keep secret," said Hannah. "At such as small school, the cadets would have noticed."

"Or, the quartermaster," said Earl. The implication hung in the air. Was that what the waste of a man had on the headmaster?

"What does this have to do with figuring out what happened to Caleb and Ridge?" asked Lisa.

"I suppose nothing, unless the rumors were true that the headmaster and Miss Kate left to become missionaries. Think about the riddle.

> *Like Paul who fled from murder a deed he did, to meet a man who unlocked a heaven's light hid,*
> *But enemies would follow him ashore, as a crown pursued a good man the more,*
> *So, Caleb and Ridge did the same, to reach an end with poor Richard's name.*
> *One will be buried in blue and the other in view.*
> *While a Shakespearean sonnet this is not, Venture to the Tempest to find the spot.*

"As a reverend, maybe the headmaster converted Caleb to become a missionary unlocking heaven's light hid. And, something happened before they left that resulted in death. Maybe Caleb, Ridge and Millie fled to Africa with the minister and poor Richard is a reference to living in poverty," said Hannah.

"But who's Richard?" asked Lisa.

"I don't know. Maybe it's the president of the mission board or something."

"What about being buried in blue and view? Could that refer to blue vestments on a foreign shore? And what about the Tempest? Could that be referring to a lethal storm on that shore?" asked Earl.

Hanna just shrugged. "I'll have to make a trip to Leigh Acres First Methodist Church. If the headmaster and any students, like Caleb, became missionaries, they would be the ones to have any records. If nothing else, they would probably have been one of their financial supporters. Normally, missionaries have to raise their own living expenses from churches and other Christians. As far as 'the Tempest,' I don't have a clue. I read the play but found it a mystery in itself. It talks about a storm and magic with a bit of romance thrown in. Nothing jumped out at me."

"Does it make a reference that could be interpreted as marking the spot in the riddle?" asked Earl.

"Not that I could see," admitted Hannah.

"The romance part points us in the right direction with Caleb and Millie," concluded Lisa.

Hannah and Earl looked at Lisa with wide-eyed anticipation, expecting a revelation from that line of thought.

"If you're expecting more, you're looking in the wrong place. That's all I've got," admitted Lisa.

They discussed the riddle a little longer and all agreed that the next step was to follow the missionary angle. So, Hannah decided to make a trip to the Leigh Acres First Methodist Church on Sunday to feel out the pastor or church secretary. Maybe they had some old records that might shed light since he had been their pastor in addition to being headmaster at the school. Approaching them casually about this subject would be less threatening than if Hannah made an official appointment. Hannah would explain honestly that she was researching his role as part of research into LaGrange Military Academy. She just wouldn't mention the part of a possible love interest.

In the early hours of the next morning, Hannah woke up with a start—still disoriented. She thought she saw a person standing in the doorway in a cadet uniform as an extension of her nightmare. In it, the cadet was being held down by others and trying to shake free. They were accusing him of being a traitor and grabbed a hot poker to brand him. Just as the branding iron clapped his skin, Hannah jerked awake. A shadow from a car's headlight moved across the wall. In her disoriented state, she took the shadow for a man.

She looked out the window as two cars seemed to stop in front of her house. After brief words through lowered windows, one went straight and the other turned around on the freshly cut grass of the cotton mill and followed. Hannah had the distinct feeling that she was the subject of their conversation. In the distance, she thought she caught a glimpse of a man's shadow by the mill as if waiting for the cars. But it was gone in a flash, so she attributed it to her imagination.

She tried to go back to sleep but finally gave up around 4:30 a.m. Since it was Sunday, she dressed for her visit to the Methodist church. She sighed, wishing it was the Presbyterian congregation with the handsome library administrator. But that was two blocks in the other direction. So, she proceeded to the Methodist enclave as planned. The old town church looked like a brick chapel found in rural France. But, it was joined at the back by a covered walkway to a two-story metal fabricated building that contained classrooms and a gym. The old church acted as the main sanctuary. As was typical of many modern churches, Hannah was struck by the lack of adornments at the altar. This was in contrast to the Presbyterian church she had just visited.

Hannah was greeted by the large crowd of people. She recognized two from the credit union, who came by and said hello. Everyone seemed genuinely happy to see her. The church was large enough to have two services so she chose the early seating, knowing that it contained primarily seniors. As such, she would feel more comfortable sitting alone among the members who sat in ones and twos, versus large families. Hannah took a spot near the back, which was also the last row with people.

The order of service was simpler with several songs followed by a lengthy sermon. It focused on a salvation message, which Hannah liked. No political positions or lecturing the congregation about bad behavior; just the simple truth of the gospel.

After the benediction, the pastor invited all new guests to the back to meet him. Hannah decided to take advantage of the offer and went. As luck would have it, she was the only visitor at the early service and had him to herself.

"I'm Hannah," she said simply, extending her hand.

"I'm Pastor Keating. I'm glad to meet you. What brought you today?" The pastor was middle aged and looked uncomfortable in his polyester suit over a dress shirt with oversized collar and wide tie that had gone out of style out several years ago. It was obvious that he wore the compulsory suit for Sunday services and was accustomed to wearing something more casual during the week. Hannah took a liking to his lack of pretention and decided to be equally transparent.

"Well, to be honest, I'm researching Reverend Ross who founded LaGrange Military Academy and I understand that he was likewise an early pastor here."

"You're correct. As a matter of fact, I did some research into church records about the man myself given his strange book entitled *Moral Living*."

"Why, is that bad?" asked Hannah.

"He had some bizarre ideas and made ridiculous arguments from a theological perspective attempting to support slavery."

"What became of him?" asked Hannah hopefully.

"It was strange. He got the church to agree to support him as a missionary to Africa. But, when they sent their tithes to the mission board, they said he never showed up."

"Really? He never went to Africa?"

"I have no idea," said the pastor with a shrug.

"Thank you for the information. And I'm sorry I didn't come today to hear the sermon exactly," said Hannah apologetically.

"Whatever your reason, I'm glad you came. We're having food today in back. Everything is homemade and some of the older members may have some knowledge of the man. Feel free to ask around."

Hannah decided to do just that and went to the grounds adjacent to the metal structure. Several picnic tables contained neatly arranged potato salad, ham, and normal picnic fare. Hannah had grown up in the proverbial "nuclear family" and didn't know that people actually made their own. She thought, *I wonder what else people make that I don't know about, like salad dressing or their own ketchup?*

Hannah sat on an extra lawn chair and was approached by two older sisters. "I heard you was investigatin' that school on the mountain," said the older of the two. She looked to be in her late eighties with white hair, wearing pants and a white sweatshirt despite the summer temperature. Her sister seemed to be half a decade younger in a more fashionable summer dress with a floral pattern.

"Yes. I've been reading some old records from the school and a cadet's journal," Hannah said, wondering how she might have heard. She had only mentioned she was researching the founding headmaster to the pastor.

"Those were some dark days," one of the old ladies said offhandedly.

Hannah reflected on the comment for a moment and asked, "You mean because the boys went off to war and died?"

"The mountain can hide dark deeds," the lady answered, seeming distracted by what food was available.

Hannah was quietly desperate to get more. "You mean the people living on the mountain?"

"No," she answered, examining the plate of ham on the table.

This was like pulling teeth. She wanted to say, *Who, then? Bigfoot, Klingons, who?*

"The good book says, 'Affliction will slay the wicked, and those who hate the righteous will be condemned,'" the old woman stated, now focused on the subject and becoming agitated.

At the sound of her rising voice, her sister stopped her from speaking more. "It's time we went home," she declared and pulled her sister away. Hannah was perplexed. *Is she crazy? Or, is there really something there that she was trying to tell me.*

Hamady watched the scene through binoculars from his perch in the second-floor lab window. Hannah's resumption of normal activities indicated that his note had had no effect and she wasn't going anywhere. So, he had to determine her next move, or place of vulnerability should he choose to simply eliminate her. The only way to do that was to watch her twenty-four-seven wherever he could. When she was home, he peered through the mill window. Other than that, he was limited to following her to and from work to see if they had haunts to catch her alone. This morning, he saw Hannah leave home and walk to the church on the other side of the tracks. That allowed him to watch her through binoculars from his second-floor lab window.

At first, he thought she was just visiting the church. She seemed to be the church type. But she stayed after the service and made a special point of talking to the Barber sisters—the only two people at the church who were connected to the family. He thought, *How could she possibly know that their grandpap supplied me and mine with "shine?"*

He stepped back and cleared his head. *She probably doesn't know anything. But if that crazy old woman talks, then the trail will lead straight to me. I'll just shut them up and nobody will be the wiser. Just a couple old ladies who died in the night. I know just the mix to make it appear that they both died from a heart attack. One in her sleep, and the other brought on by finding her sister dead. It's so simple.*

Chapter 23
The Grave

At work the next day, Hannah's phone rang. It was Earl. Hannah had told Earl and Lisa about the church visit and the strange reference by one of the elderly sisters about dark deeds on the mountain. As a result, Earl planned to call his dad to see if he could tap his friends on the mountain to find out more.

"EJ did some checking. It's a little stranger than we thought. His friend on the mountain said there's a 'haint' (ghost) that haunts the graveyard."

"You can't be serious. In this day and age?" said an incredulous Hannah.

"That's right. And there's more. They claim the haint's a man from the school who emanates from a strangely marked grave. It's marked by a nameless headstone that reads, 'May these three souls who saw violence at death find eternal peace.'"

"You're kidding," said Hannah. "So there was some dark deed on the mountain? Do you think it's Caleb, Millie, and Ridge?"

"Maybe," said Earl.

"But how would we find out? It's not like we can exhume the bodies and compare the DNA to the families. They would never agree to that."

"Maybe there's another way," commented Earl.

"What way is that?" asked Hannah hopefully.

"I'm guessing that if folks took the time to bury them with a headstone, there must have been some care taken. It wasn't like somebody tried to hide the bodies.

I believe it was customary to bury people in their finest clothes. In the case of a cadet, it would have been a uniform. For Millie, a dress."

"But who would have buried them?" asked Hannah. "If they were murdered, you'd think that whoever did it would have hidden the bodies and buried them in the woods or threw them in the river."

"Story has it that the mountain folk did it, and it wasn't one of their own. They did it because they wanted to let the dead rest in peace."

"But, we still can't get permission to exhume the bodies. For one thing, we don't have any evidence to present to a family or a coroner."

"I think it's more of a quiet DIY project. You like DIY, don't you?" asked Earl.

"Not that kind of DIY," said Hannah with a shudder. Then, she came up with an idea. "I tell you what: I was going to interview the headmaster's great-grandniece who you found in your phone calls. As uncomfortable as that will be, it's still preferable to digging up dead people. If she tells me where he went, and it turns out that he took Caleb, Ridge, and Millie with him, it will eliminate our need to dig."

"That's a long shot. And besides, digging up a grave don't sound so bad compared to what I do every day. Have you ever worked on a bad septic tank?" asked Earl

"I haven't, and I hope I never will," said Hannah. "One thing's for sure, the mountain people must have good hearts to try to right a wrong and bury the two," said Hannah.

"Not necessarily," said Earl. "I said they wanted the dead to rest in peace, not necessarily right a wrong. They may have seen an omen and assigned it to that event. So a burial may have been intended to ward off a haunting or some other evil."

"What's an omen?"

"Out here in the country, you hear and see strange things," explained Earl. "It's hard not to get a chill when you recognize a sign of something unnatural."

"Can you give me an example?" asked Hannah.

Earl recited a few.

1) If a robin with a red breast flies into the house, death is near.

2) If a seemingly broken clock suddenly chimes, death is near. On a related note, never stop a clock in a room where a death occurred; that may bring on bad luck.

3) If somebody dies in your home, open all windows so the spirit may move on. Also, be sure to cover the mirrors, not looking at yourself while doing so. The next person to see themselves in a mirror with a deceased person present will die next.

4) Pregnant women walking on the grave immediately after the funeral will give birth to a child with a clubfoot.

5) Never have your picture taken with a person standing on either side of you. The person in the middle will die next.

6) Never be the last person buried in a cemetery or your spirit will be required to stay and watch over the others.

Earl showed no sign of stopping, so Hannah interjected. "No one knows the time and hour of their death or can forestall God's plan," she said, referencing Ecclesiastes. "People most definitely don't know when their time will come. Like fish tragically caught in a net or like birds trapped in a snare, so are human beings caught in a time of tragedy that suddenly falls to them."

Earl's succinct reply was, "Maybe so, but it can't hurt."

To lighten the mood, Hannah expounded on an illogical practice of her own. "Did I ever tell you why we never went to midnight mass when I was a kid? My dad said that robbers patrolled the streets looking for people who went to church and stole their presents."

"You didn't believe him, did you?" laughed Earl.

"Actually, I did. It should have dawned on me that we only went to church once a year, and this was his way of justifying to my mother why he didn't want to go. But to this day, I always look out the window suspiciously and check the locks twice on Christmas Eve."

"So," added Earl in triumph, "you've got a couple superstitions of your own. You can see why these things die hard."

"I can," admitted Hannah. "I'd love to visit the graves anyway to write down some of the epitaphs from the headstones. They might be interesting."

Earl verbally warned her over the phone, "Never collect epithets from gravestones. Otherwise, you'll lose your memory."

Hannah waited for a snicker, announcing it was a joke. None came. So Hannah said, "Thanks for the education, Earl."

"Always happy to help the ignorant," replied Earl again. Still no sign of being a joke. So, Hannah said goodbye and hung up.

Chapter 24
The Flower Shop

Hannah went home and fed the cats, then walked over to see Lisa and Earl. Earl had given her the headmaster's descendant's name, Margaret Waters, but didn't have her contact information handy. So, Hannah made arrangements to get it later. She found Lisa putting icepacks on Earl's feet.

"What going on?"

"It's my feet acting up again. I was told that I may have nerve damage from standing too long," said Earl.

"Did the doctor say they can do anything?" asked Hannah with a pained look on her face.

"He says to stay off my feet and see a specialist. I can't rightly do that and pay the bills, can I?" said Earl sullenly.

Hannah didn't reply. What could she say?

"So, Earl. You mentioned you could give me the address of Margaret Waters, the minister's great-grandniece. Do you have that?"

"Oh, yes. She owns the flower shop," said Earl. "Let me get the number."

"Now wait. You mean the flower shop right there?" asked Hannah, pointing. It was practically next to her house.

"Yes. Didn't I mention that?" asked Earl.

"No," said Hannah and Lisa in unison.

"I thought you'd just call her there," said Earl defensively.

"I'll visit," said Hannah.

"I'll go with you," said Earl. "Remember how your last in-person interview went with the doctor's descendent?"

"I can handle it this time. Besides, I'm a churchgoer. She might be thrown off if you show up."

"I should be insulted, but I see what you mean. I'll just wait for you to report back," conceded Earl. He was in pain and had no desire to argue the point.

Between work inspections, Hannah entered the flower shop. She was disappointed to find that the owner was away attending the funerals of two elderly women who suddenly passed away at her church. Hannah was reminded of the two elderly sisters she had recently met, but just as quickly forgot them. That would be too much of a coincidence.

She returned later in the day and found the owner behind the counter. Now, maybe she could determine the fate of the headmaster from his descendent.

"Can I help you?" asked the woman behind the counter. She looked a little like Mrs. Garrett from the show *The Facts of Life*, but with a few less miles.

"I was looking for a basic arrangement for a woman at work."

"For what occasion?" she asked.

"Just a work anniversary. Something in the $40 range," Hannah guessed. In fact, there was no woman at work and she had no idea of what flowers really cost. She just didn't want to go home with something filled with teddy bears or fake flowers and a balloon. She really wanted information.

"I have something I can create tomorrow. Will that work?" she said, pulling out an order slip.

"That would be fine," said Hannah. As Hannah was slowly filling out the slip, she casually asked, "I hear that you're the descendent of the Reverend Peabody

Ross, the headmaster at LaGrange Military Academy. Is that right?" Unfortunately, the question came out clunky and somewhat suspicious.

"Yes," Margaret said without elaboration.

Hannah continued, "So, do you know what became of him? I thought he became a missionary in Africa but it appears that the missionary society didn't have any records of his departure."

"Well, I don't know why not. He was a great preacher and went onto serve in the Dark Continent," she said defensively. Hannah was a little surprised at the term "Dark Continent," which was probably politically incorrect even before she was born.

"I must have missed it," said Hannah, slowly filling out the form. "He was close to his assistant who went with him—is that right?"

"What assistant?" she shot back.

"Miss Kate. I believe she was an African-American woman, sort of a caretaker at the school," said Hannah.

"What are you implying? He didn't go off with no slave woman to Louisiana, or Africa, or nowhere else," she said in a shrill voice.

"Sorry," said Hannah, trying to act indifferent. "I was just making conversation. I'm sure he did the world a great service in Africa for a very long time. Did he ever write back to the family with any interesting stories? Or anything to the mission board that was of interest? I understand that missionaries had to write progress reports for their support organization."

She just stared with a scowl. "If he did, I wouldn't share the letters with you or anyone else. I'll have your flowers ready tomorrow after 5 p.m. Is there nothing else?"

Hannah said no and meekly exited whereupon she bumped into Hamady peering through the flower shop window. She barely recognized him having only seen him once at a distance in sunglasses. She recalled that Earl had mentioned him in passing as being a descendent of the merchant who had supplied the quartermaster at the school. It was a loose lead, but a lead all the same.

"I'm sorry, Mr. Hamady. I'm Hannah Sparrow from the credit union. Oddly enough, I was hoping to make an appointment with you some time to ask about your family."

"I don't know nothing. Stay away from me and mine`." He thereupon promptly walked off.

Hannah thought that the only thing worse than his manners was his grammar.... *He certainly doesn't express himself very well.*

To top it off, Hannah got a text from her boss, Clyde Higgins at the credit union. He wanted to see her in his office right away. *This can't be good,* she thought.

When she arrived, he shut the door.

"I now understand that you've been harassing Margaret Waters at the flower shop," Clyde said accusingly.

"I would hardly call it harassment. I asked her a couple questions about what ever happened to her great-uncle, the headmaster at LaGrange College. I didn't even know she was a customer."

"She's not a customer, but I don't want you speaking to her anyway."

Now Hannah was mad. "If she's not a customer, what right do you have to dictate what private conversations I have with my own neighbors?"

Clyde stuttered something, but Hannah cut him off. "Let me make one thing clear. Making comments about how I conduct my personal life clearly creates a hostile work environment. If you ever challenge me again, I'll sue so fast your head will spin."

"I have every right to protect the credit union's reputation," responded Clyde.

"If you think so, I invite you to talk to human resources right now. In fact, I'll do it for you," said Hannah as she got up to leave. She was mad and sweating. As a result, her glasses had slid down her nose. But she fought the urge to push them up, wanting to leave with her head high without displaying her nerdy habit.

"Now wait," objected Clyde. "There's no need for that. I'll drop it this time, but if I catch you doing it to a customer, that will be another thing."

Hannah didn't bother responding. She just left.

Back in his grandfather's mixing room, Hamady paced the floor. He was normally careful of all the equipment and neatly arranged ingredients lest he lose precious money. But he couldn't stop himself. He wildly threw beakers in all directions. Then he paused to have a conversation with himself like the madman he was becoming.

"I thought that killing the old ladies would stop her learning about my family. Now she's asking more questions. What should I do now?"

"You obviously have to kill her too."

"But what if they figure out it was me?"

"If you don't, they'll arrest you anyway and probably figure out you killed the old women."

"I can't just go over there and kill her at her house."

"Then kill her somewhere else like the little library or the LaGrange Academy ruins. Nobody will suspect you."

The conversation over, he smiled at the plan. It would be over soon.

Chapter 25
The Feed Association

That night, Hannah, Earl, and Lisa decided to have dinner in the neighboring town of Moulton for a change of scenery. Moulton had two steak restaurants and everyone in the county was divided on their favorite. You were faithful to one or the other, but never both. It was like the Alabama and Auburn rivalry. Hannah didn't personally care; she just didn't want to eat from the salad bar at either...just a bacon double cheeseburger and onion rings. They didn't have any Cheetos.

As they ate, Hannah debriefed on the flower shop meeting. "So, what did she mean about 'not running off with no slave woman in Louisiana or Africa'? I never mentioned Louisiana," asked a confused Hannah.

"Now that I think of it, I vaguely recall a rumor that some local pastor went off to Louisiana under unusual circumstances involving a woman. I didn't think it was him, but it could be. Maybe the woman he took was Miss Kate. At the time, New Orleans was more a portal to the world and fairly progressive. He might have gotten away with setting up house with an African woman. But, I suspect that even New Orleans wasn't that liberal," said Earl.

"So, that's why people thought Louisiana instead of Africa?" said Hannah, still confused. "You'd think that his whereabouts would come to light eventually if he was that close."

"I suspect that people didn't believe any man from around here was 'that holy.' They were more inclined to think he took contributions and went to Louisiana instead. Maybe he changed his name? You can understand the rumors. He left suddenly. She was likewise gone and there was nobody's word other than his family's to say he went to Africa. Their silence after he left with no further word about his work, or even his demise at the hand of the natives, left people wondering if it really happened."

"I guess that's a dead end. If he just ran off to Louisiana, I don't see that there's any connection with Caleb, Ridge and Millie," concluded Lisa.

"To make things doubly worse, that florist called old Clyde at the bank," lamented Hannah.

"She didn't?!" exclaimed Lisa.

"She did," said Hannah, who then described the meeting, ending with, "Old Clyde can set things up to get me fired for reasons not having anything to do with my threatening him with going to HR about a hostile work environment. I shouldn't have lost my temper."

"Just let it cool down," said Earl.

"Maybe you should go to HR about a hostile environment to make it official right now," overrode Lisa. She was ready for a fight.

"But it's not really that clear. He never said anything about my gender, religion, or anything else clearly illegal. He can claim he was protecting the credit union. It's really a gray area," said Hannah with a dejected look.

"I see what you mean. I guess you should just let it cool down. Hopefully you put a scare into him and it will die. But that really burns me up," concluded Lisa.

"But that leads to another issue," said Hannah. "We certainly can't dig up the bodies on the mountain. Clyde would have my head for that."

"Not if we did it at night. Nobody would know," countered Earl.

"Really? Dig up corpses at night?" exclaimed Hannah, drawing the interest of fellow diners.

One of the diners to look up despite his attempt to stay incognito at the bar was Hamady. Up to that point, he couldn't hear a thing and thought the evening was a complete bust. But this new turn had real possibilities. They were obviously thinking of making a trip to the LaGrange Academy ruins cemetery. For all he knew, Hannah was planning to test the bodies for drug overdoses caused by the family business. Whatever the reason, the cemetery was a perfect place for an ambush—if she was alone. All he had to do was follow her there. With a smile, he slipped off the bar stool and out the door.

Earl interjected in a lower voice, "I'm serious about the corpses. But I have another thought. After our last discussion, I made a couple calls about the quartermaster's descendent."

"You mean Miller, the president of the Seed Association," replied Hannah.

"Yep, that's the one. I can't say the apple fell far from the tree."

"What does that have to do with digging up corpses?" asked Lisa.

"I'm thinking that if anybody would openly brag about their family killing a cadet, it's them. Maybe we get lucky and he admits that his great-granddad killed Ridge and Caleb to protect the supply scheme. Then, we have our answer and there's no more digging, no pun intended," said Earl proudly. He was proud of the pun more than the plan.

"But, that sounds like a respectable job. Are you sure the apple fell far from the tree?" asked Hannah in surprise.

"You would think so, wouldn't you? But there's always been talk that what should be a nonprofit organization ain't so much," confided Earl.

"How's that? You're saying he's profiting from it?" said Hannah, not knowing the first thing about farming. She only knew about construction and land valuation.

"It all has to do with drying corn. Basically, farmers schedule their corn to be taken to the Feed Association to have the moisture removed in a huge dehydration machine. That way, it can be stored and used for feed and such," explained Earl.

"That sounds reasonable. What's the scam?" said Hannah, trying to show her command of street lingo.

Earl paused and smiled at her feeble attempt. It was like somebody from a foreign country trying to use popular slang. "Well, at harvest time, the farmers need this to happen fast and not have their corn sitting in the fields waiting for their scheduled time."

"Let me guess," interrupted Hannah. "In order to get a good processing time, they have to make a personal deal under the table with the Feed Association president. Otherwise, their corn rots in the fields."

"You got it," confirmed Earl. "At least that's the rumor. But nobody's really talking because they don't want to be on the bad side of the Feed Association."

"So, we're thinking that he's carried on the tradition set by his great-granddad, which was passed down from generation to generation?" asked Hannah.

"I know he did," said Lisa, suddenly recalling an incident. "A girlfriend of mine in high school rebuffed him, and her dad's crops were mysteriously bumped on the pickup schedule and half his corn rotted in the field." She grimaced in disgust. "To make matters worse, Justin bragged about it."

"See," said Earl, "if we can get his dad to brag about his kin killing a cadet or two, we have an end to our mystery."

"There's only one problem," said Hannah. "The Feed Association has big accounts with the Credit Union. If I ask him, Clyde Higgins will have my job for sure. That's almost worse than digging up the grave."

"Not if I do it," said Lisa.

"You?" exclaimed Hannah and Earl in unison.

"Yes. My company supplies parts to the Feed Association for their machinery. I make an excuse to deliver some parts and a gift from the manufacturing plant to the President. In the process, I make idle chitchat and ask him," said Lisa.

"I know you can use your cute southern accent on Yankees up north, but he'll see right through it," objected Earl.

"So what if he does? If the gift is good enough, he won't care. He'll think he got the upper hand anyway," said Lisa, pleased with herself.

Earl looked at Hannah and smiled. "It could work. And if it doesn't, we can always dig up the corpses."

Chapter 26
Lisa and the Feed Association

Lisa approached the corrugated building flanked by corn dryers and a seed chute. Large farm equipment was interspersed haphazardly throughout the gravel lot in front and behind the building. She took care to park as close as possible to the entrance lest she get sideswiped by a machine or its swinging appendage.

Lisa approached the president's secretary. She looked every bit the administrative equivalent of a trophy for the executive. She wore an expensive miniskirt and low-cut silk blouse that accentuated her ample bosom, courtesy of a big-city plastic surgeon. "Hi, Sylvia. Long time no see."

"Lisa. I haven't seen you since, well, never mind," Sylvia said, blushing. "What can I do for you?"

"I was hoping to see Mr. Miller. I have a gift for him from the plant," said Lisa.

"Sure. Let me make sure he's free."

Lisa stood in the lobby for only a moment. The prospect of a gift was a universal way to gain entrance.

After some small talk where Lisa expressed the parts plant's appreciation for his support, Lisa ventured into her reason for coming. "Like I was saying," continued Lisa, "I'm an amateur historian and I was reading a cadet's journal and found your great-grandfather a colorful figure at the school."

"Great-granddad was that. He started the family business and helped the school and the Confederacy in the process."

"And what business was that?" asked Lisa.

"Well, Great-granddad was in a number of enterprises from being a 'sutler' after the war started (merchant who followed the Confederate Army to sell goods to the soldiers) to trading in 'fairy boats' to the soldiers at Fredericksburg (spelled *fairy* due to their miniature size)."

Lisa assumed that tossing out the terms "sutler" and "fairy boats" was intended to test her claim of being a history nut. She was clearly flunking because she had no idea what they meant.

Later, Hannah explained, "Before the battle of Fredericksburg, there was a lull in the fighting across the Rappahannock River while the Union Army waited for a core of engineers to bring up pontoon bridges from the rear. Both sides settled into a kind of unofficial ceasefire. The soldiers weren't allowed to fraternize, so they took it upon themselves to float little boats constructed from anything, including shell casings filled with items of trade. The Confederate soldiers, for example, had plenty of tobacco, but no coffee. The Yankees had just the opposite. So it was said that 'the waters were fairly dotted with the fairy fleet,' for several days until the fighting resumed."

But that didn't help Lisa here and now with the Feed Association president.

"And when it resumed, old Bobby Lee gave the Yankees a beating," added the president who looked out of place with his expensive suit that did little to disguise his pudgy frame. He leered at Lisa to see if she would expound on the event. She couldn't. But she could put him on the defensive.

"So, your great-grandfather traded with the Yankees?" asked Lisa, leaning forward with the physical dominance used in her high school basketball years to intimidate.

"He was just getting the comforts of home for our southern boys," he retorted smugly, refusing to move even the slightest.

"So, how did he get the money to set up in business in the first place?" asked Lisa, raising the ante. They both knew he was as "crooked as a Virginia fence."

"He was an honest and industrious man. He saved his money."

Lisa tried switching to southern charm. "Your family has done well and is a good example for the kids around Leigh Acres, that's for sure."

"Thank you," he replied triumphantly.

"I believe he also supported farmers on the mountain by acquiring materials on their behalf from school supplies. Maybe that's how he got started in business," commented Lisa. She tried to say it nicely, but it was clear that she said he was stealing from the school and selling it.

His smile faded. "What makes you say that?"

"One of the cadet's journals mentioned helping unload wagons after dark and routing part of the shipment to local farmers for 'storage.'" Lisa reinforced the word "storage" with finger quotes to indicate the cadet recognized the lie.

"Your cadet was obviously incorrect, and I don't appreciate any implications otherwise."

Lisa decided to lay it on the line. There was a reason she got parts through to suppliers. After finesse failed, go with the direct approach. "That cadet disappeared, and I was wondering if your family lore had any thoughts on what happened to him."

"If you don't mind, I have a call to make. You can show yourself out."

Sometimes the direct approach just makes things worse.

Recapping the conversation with Hannah and Earl in the driveway, they all agreed that the interviews were going nowhere.

Not long after, Lisa's cell phone rang. It was her boss. All Hannah and Earl could hear were her responses to whatever was being said on the other side.

"No, I wasn't slandering one of our best customers.... No, sir. I was simply making conversation after explaining how much we appreciated his business.... No, sir, I was just trying to settle some questions left in a cadet's journal from LaGrange Academy.... No, that girl from the credit union didn't put me up to it."

Hannah flinched at the reference. "Was everyone around here connected and out to get her?"

After a few "yes, sirs" and "no, sirs," Lisa hung up.

They decided it was time to cool it on interviews before Hannah *and* Lisa both got fired, or worse.

But *worse* was already in the works as Hamady walked the grounds of LaGrange Academy. As he suspected, everywhere on the grounds seemed to make a stealthy approach too difficult. He turned to the graveyard with all its headstones and shadows. It would be the perfect place to kill her. Now he just had to find the weapon of choice.

Chapter 27
Midnight in the Graveyard

Hannah couldn't help herself and looked online to search for tips for visiting graveyards. She reasoned that there were "how to" videos and thoughts on just about everything, so why not that? It turned out that there was. Beyond the macabre that she discarded, there was one comment she found of real value. It was a reminder that each headstone represented the hopes, dreams, and fears of a real person with a real family. "We should walk away from the visit with the intention of living each day to the fullest and never take for granted our relationships with others, even if you have a family of fruit loops."

That night, Hannah, Earl, and Lisa parked in front of the white gates of LaGrange Military Academy. It was a crescent moon, which made Hannah feel a little better.

To lighten the mood, Hannah felt the need to impart historical trivia. "Did you know that Robert Louis Stevenson was inspired to write *Dr. Jekyll and Mr. Hyde* based on a real man, William Brodie?"

"Why are you telling us this now?" asked Earl.

"Just trying to help the ignorant. And besides, the moon's almost full," answered Hannah honestly. "It made me think of it."

"Oh" was all they could say as they made their way through the ghostly specter of evening shadows, sights, and sounds.

Hannah continued, "In eighteenth-century Scotland, this Brodie was a respectable man and head of the trade guilds. He was also wealthy due to a lavish inheritance with multiple houses and businesses. But he was a gambler and ran up debts to some dubious lenders. So, he met up with a man named George Smith and they turned into quite the pair of ruffians. They robbed homes and businesses quite successfully until they got too greedy and tried to rob Scotland itself of its treasury with their gang that now numbered four. They failed and went into hiding. Fortunately, the authorities offered a reward and one of the gang turned in the others. They were convicted in a trial widely covered by the press. They say that over forty thousand people attended his hanging. So, the sight of a respectable man that turned into a ruffian at night inspired *Dr. Jekyll and Mr. Hyde*."

"I see," said Earl, watching the edges of their illuminated path. "Glad he wasn't from around here."

"Closer to home, some of our founding fathers were Jekyll and Hyde types. John Hancock was a respectable man by day and a smuggler by night. John Paul Jones was said to have killed a man before leaving Britain for the colonies and switching sides. And don't forget Ben Franklin. He was a mild-mannered printer that transformed into a mad scientist with his 'fly a kite in a lightning storm' gig. They were all friends, just like Brodie and Smith, you know. Jones even named a ship after Franklin, called it the *Bonhomme Home Richard*."

"Still, they weren't from around here," responded Earl, never removing his gaze from the path's edges.

"Caleb and the rest of the boys would have studied them; that makes them somewhat from around here," countered Hannah. "That still doesn't give you any pause to think?"

"What gives me pause is that when I was a kid up here, I saw the biggest snake in my life when I was riding a mini bike on this path. It literally came after me *and* the bike," commented Earl without stopping his head from scanning side to side.

Hannah's eyes became as big as pie pans and she stopped talking, lest she interrupt Earl's concentration.

Earl suddenly stopped and held up his finger to be silent.

Hamady stood frozen and out of sight on the path behind. He had accidently clanged the axe he'd taken from the closed dry goods store against a rock. He stopped in his tracks, not making a sound. He was already frustrated that Earl had come along, hoping that it would be just the two women. And now, Earl was the one vigilant for potential danger, making it doubly worse. Still, *that woman* might wander off or lag behind, giving Hamady the opportunity to kill her and slip back into the woods, Earl or no Earl.

"What is it?" whispered Lisa.

"I could have sworn I heard something in the woods," Earl whispered back.

"Like an animal?" whispered Hannah as her eyes darted into the shadows.

"No. Like a person," said Earl.

After standing frozen for another fifteen seconds, Earl laughed. "There's nobody out there. It's just Hannah's stories about Jekyll and Hyde getting to me. What are the chances of being stalked by a mild-mannered businessman turned madman with a lab?"

They all laughed and continued on. It was almost dark when they finally entered the little graveyard. The tombstones sometimes stood proudly erect, but most were bowing at all angles from neglect. All stood in silence like a sea of dead. Most were overgrown and covered in moss. It was obvious that even their mourners had long ago been buried themselves in this remote outpost.

Hannah was nervous. An old habit she picked up as a teenager in this situation was to ask questions and make jokes. "What pithy saying would you put on your headstone? Something like, 'I told you I was sick'?"

Lisa chuckled. "How about, 'Does this coffin make my butt look big?'"

Not to be outdone, Earl countered with, "I asked for a pyramid and all I got was this lousy rock."

No amount of jokes made their little plan any easier. They stopped at the grave in front of the stone marked "May these three souls that saw violence at death find eternal peace" and began to dig. It was more than half an hour when they finally hit the top of rotting wood. With gloves on, they pulled off the loose wooden slats and stripped away the dirt that had fallen between the cracks. They were expecting to find two cadet skeletons in period uniforms and a girl. Instead, there were two adults and a baby.

"I don't understand," said Hannah, leaning back in the hole.

Earl lightly brushed the dirt off the garments and found a black robe on one skeleton with a cross. The other skeleton had a dress. Most distressing was the little dress adorning the infant.

Finally, Hannah pieced it together. "The black gown appears to be ministerial robes—a vestment."

"So, the other corpse is Miss Kate and the infant is obviously their baby. The tombstone was a label, 'May these three souls that saw violence at death find eternal peace.' It contained a mother and child lost in the violence of childbirth," concluded Earl.

Earl and Hannah climbed out of the hole and sat on the grass with Lisa contemplating all the implications. "The headmaster had a love child with Miss Kate, his mistress."

"Maybe he was so distraught that he killed himself," added Lisa.

"I can only assume that the mountain folk took pity on them and decided to go along with the story that they went to Africa as missionaries. They quietly buried them here as a little family," conjectured Hannah.

"That would make sense. The people on the little hill farms certainly weren't slave owners. They may have been sympathetic with the two who couldn't marry due to the constraints of society," said Lisa with a sigh.

"How sad," observed Hannah. "It's too bad he was so conflicted not only with society but within himself. He published an argument supporting slavery yet loved a slave. I suppose he's not the first person, given that Samuel Clemens wrote a whole book about the same conflict."

"Should I know Samuel Clemens?" asked Earl.

"Sorry. You know him by his pen name, Mark Twain. In his work *Huckleberry Finn*, Huck spends most of the book trying to reconcile his efforts to help his friend, Jim, escape from slavery, with Huck's hatred for abolitionists he learned from society. In the end, Huck discards society in favor of helping his friend."

They sat for a few more moments in silence before filling the hole again. Earl and Lisa started toward the truck when Hannah stopped and said, "You go on ahead. I'll be right behind you after I say a brief prayer for the little family."

Hamady's heart skipped as he finally saw an opportunity to get the woman alone. He silently edged within reach from his spot behind a large headstone where he'd been standing for the entire dig. His eyes became enlarged with glee as he raised the axe, waiting for Earl and Lisa to depart. He needed just a few more seconds. Then, they'd be far enough away to complete his task.

Earl and Lisa slowed, then stopped. They looked at each other, then said to Hannah, "Unless you feel strongly about being alone, we'd rather stay and do it together. We'll each say something."

Hannah gladly agreed, and the three gathered next to the grave, where Hannah spoke first, followed by Earl, and then Lisa, each becoming increasingly choked up as they went. They concluded with a few moments of silence, then began their long walk to the truck.

Hamady swore to himself as he followed closely behind, waiting for any opportunity to kill her, but none came. In the end, he watched with silent fury as the truck pulled out with his prey tucked safely inside.

"So, where does that leave us?" asked Lisa as they approached the house.

"The cadets weren't buried anywhere on the mountain, I'm sure of it. There's no other graves with the telltale signs of not belonging to a local family. I guess we're back to the riddle and investigating our remaining suspects."

"You mean back to interviews?" observed Lisa.

"I'll take one last look at the vault to see if I missed anything. If I can't find anything, it's back to the interviews," said Hannah.

"But this time, I do the talking," interjected Earl.

"I suppose so," agreed Hannah. "You're the only one left who isn't about to lose their job."

"The question is," said Earl, "how do I approach Mr. Swanson, the only remaining descendent to be questioned about his ancestor—Millie's father? We don't exactly circulate in the same social circles."

The Swansons had come up in the world and were now the local gentry. They were the closest thing to modern-day plantation owners. Even their house on the farm looked like George Washington's Mount Vernon. Given the dismal results from the other interviews, the threesome had to think of some way to approach.

Chapter 28
The Vault

Hannah arrived at the library just before closing. Bert said she was welcome to stay and do her research if she closed the door on her departure. Bert said he'd swing by later and set the deadbolt.

If Hannah thought the vault was spooky before, it was doubly so being alone in the library. So, she went to work looking through other old boxes, trying to find anything having to do with the Union. As she was in the last box, the door behind her slammed shut and the light switch outside the vault turned off.

Hannah's heart raced in the dark, the only dim light emitting only from her penlight. Luckily, she carried one for harder-to-find documents in the deep recesses of boxes. She was breathing hard and perspiring from having yelled for five minutes. She had to settle down and think.

She scanned the walls behind the shelving. Luckily, this wasn't like an old-fashioned vault with metal sides. She knew from the modern bank branch that only the front door was metal, making the customers feel secure about their valuables. Actually, it was a simple room often enclosed with drywall. In this case, it had originally been a temporary vault while the burned bank was relocated. *Think, Hannah, is this building wood or cement block?* Her mind went back to the outside. To her disappointment, she remembered that it was cement block.

She sat for a minute and scanned the room with the light. That meant that she either had to find a way out through an internal wall leading to the library or the ceiling. She looked up and saw the asbestos tiles suspended in a network of metal rods like most Americans' basements. Could it be that simple?

Hannah tested the shelves and found them to be solid enough to climb the nine feet to the ceiling. She pushed up a tile to reveal an open attic. She coughed from the decades-old dust now disturbed. Hannah could see the header board atop the two-by-four studs capping the interior walls well enough to place her knees for support. She made her way a few feet to the interior room.

She was about to drop through to get out and into clean air when it occurred to her the culprit could be inside in case of her escape. She flicked off her light and quietly lifted a tile to peak into the library. From this vantage point, she could make out a person standing in the dark.

Hamady was exceedingly pleased with himself. He thought, *She stopped making noise and obviously gave up. That old vault is small, and the library is due to be closed tomorrow and the next day. There's no way she can last more than a day. She'll either die due to a lack of oxygen or dehydration. Either way, the problem will be gone. I just have to watch the street and make sure that nobody is around who can see me slip out.*

Hannah saw that the man was just standing there frozen by the front window. Was it somebody who intended her harm and hoped she'd suffocate, or just a friend of Bert's who saw the lights left on after closing and who'd secured the vault door? Hannah decided to play it safe and remained perfectly still until the man left. After what seemed like an eternity, he opened the front door and exited the library.

After waiting five more minutes, Hannah made her way to an outer wall, where she could drop onto the old card catalogue. Her feet were partially asleep from kneeling on the narrow board, and she was afraid she'd break a bone from landing on the concrete floor.

After a few muffled coughs from the dust, she made it from the ceiling to the cabinet and the floor. Hannah opened the door and peaked onto the street. All was quiet. She debated where to go next and decided on Lisa's house. She would know what to do.

"What happened?" said Lisa, looking at Hannah, covered in dust with a raspy voice from coughing. Hannah slowed down and explained again about being locked in, her would-be jailer, and her escape.

They sat and thought about the answer.

"It could be that we're getting close to solving the mystery. But more likely, it was just a friend of Bert's who thought he was doing a good deed," observed Earl.

Lisa nodded in agreement.

"But what about the note left in my mailbox just the other day?" objected Hannah.

"I don't think they're related. Nobody around here would try to hurt you because of our little research. I really think it was just a passing old man who closed up what he thought was an empty library," said Earl in a consoling voice.

After a little more discussion, they all agreed. Nevertheless, Earl would double his vigilance on watching Hannah's home and Hannah wouldn't frequent any more vaults.

Chapter 29
Dream House

Hannah was beginning to wonder if she should just give up. Then, on the way back from a construction inspection, she saw an auction sign go up on a country property about two miles out on the county road outside of Leigh Acres. She had noticed the property on multiple occasions. On it stood an old farmhouse between two fields with rows of trees lining the long one hundred-yard driveway that looked like a royal path to a castle. The yard was unkempt with several years between grass cuttings, but the house itself had three pillars on a front porch that represented what Hannah considered the quintessential southern postcard. It appeared that some people had rented it recently and left, presumably before the house was sold out from under them. Then, an idea came to her. She rushed home and found Lisa and Earl next door, having just arrived from work.

"Have you seen all the parcel signs around the county?"

"Yes," confirmed Earl. "They say it's supposed to be the biggest land sale since before the war."

"The Civil War?" asked Hannah.

They both laughed. "World War II," came the answer. Hannah felt offended. There were quite a few wars since that time.

"Why? Are you interested in becoming a land baron or something?" asked Lisa.

"No," said Hannah. "It's a way for Earl to talk to Old Man Swanson. Do you know the antebellum home on the county highway that's in the auction?"

"The one with all the trees on the way to Town Creek?" asked Lisa with an encroaching look of skepticism.

"Yes."

"It's on five acres and is its own parcel," confirmed Earl. "I see where you're going with this. All the parcels are strictly farmland except that one. If we go to the auction and bid on it, we have an excuse to mosey on over to Old Man Swanson like one of the boys. He'll surely be there to buy up the other parcels."

"I love that house," confirmed Hannah, picturing the house in her mind. She could see herself enjoying the huge yard with rows of trees. Maybe even fence it and get a horse. Plus, she'd be rid of whoever was after her, if they were after her, by moving. The only downside was that it was not near Earl and Lisa. Almost reading her mind, Lisa said, "It ain't but the next town over."

Hannah thought about it. She was a banker after all. She could get qualified, own her dream home, and solve the mystery, or at least be out of harm's way.

The next day, Hannah called the phone number listed on one of the local parcels and found out that you had to have a preapproval letter from a bank up to the amount of your bid along with $1,000 to hold the parcel if you won. Hannah figured that getting preapproved for $50,000 might be more than enough. She was getting excited about owning such a quaint home and went to inspect the property.

Hannah drove up the path that had once been a gravel driveway. Now, it was more like a trail lined by tall grass flanked by a row of skeletal trees on either side. Hannah's little truck approached the house, which peaked sheepishly behind overgrown shrubs. The formerly white pillars of a porch marked the front corners of the house despite years of grime. Hannah stopped, turned off her engine, and listened for any sounds of a dog or other possible threat. The only sound was that of a spring breeze rustling the newly blooming trees to create the only break in the silence.

Hannah tenderly stepped on the front board of the porch, which had sporadic holes and cracks. A fear entered her mind that if she crashed through into the basement below, nobody would hear her cries for help, assuming she was still conscious. She tested each board that groaned under her weight as she slid toward the front door as if on a skin of thin ice over a lake. She made it to the door only to find it padlocked with a crudely added latch on top of the old door. Hannah retraced her steps back to the front steps as if attempting a retreat from a mine field.

She made her way around an old path with grass and moss separating each stone worn smooth by generations of families. She opened a withered iron gate that served as the opening into the garden. It was now a garden in name only. An apple tree in the center had previously served as the jeweled center point but now just looked sadly withdrawn by its dilapidated surroundings. The bark had a sort of creeping shadow of moss that seemed somehow unhealthy even to look upon. Hannah stopped once again to listen for any danger that lurked in the tall kudzu that advanced like a cancer on the house.

Hannah made her way to a back porch of brick that looked sturdy enough. She tried the door and found it unlocked, or broken. Either way, it opened with a scream of the hinges and Hannah entered what was the kitchen. It was getting toward dusk and the house seemed almost like a Venus fly trap waiting for its next victim. The kitchen had cheap cabinets with no sort of design in their placement, obviously added for renters to have the minimum requirements to elicit a lease. Hannah moved to the dining room, which had a high, ornate ceiling of decorative molding interspersed with falling plaster from what seemed like water damage.

The attached living room featured a large fireplace like you would see in the last scene of an Agatha Christie film where all suspects nervously waited for the affable Miss Marple to name the killer. Light entered through a wall of windows overlooking the front porch that had successfully repelled Hannah's first attempt at entry. Dreary wooden floors creaked, making Hannah stop to make sure they weren't the sounds of footsteps of some serial-killing vagrant inhabiting the house. Hearing nothing and anxious to leave, Hannah made her way through three side bedrooms, each with its own Victorian fireplace and a bathroom that looked like it had been in the center of the World War II Dresden air raid.

Hannah stopped as she heard a car approach and stop next to her truck. She made her way quickly, thinking that it might be the county sheriff investigating a prowler reported by the farmer a quarter mile up the road. Then she heard, "Hannah, you there?"

"Yeah, Earl. I'm around back in the kitchen."

Hannah made her way to the back door, where she met Earl and Lisa. "You said you were going to check out this place. So, we swung by while coming back from Town Creek and initially thought you weren't here. Then, we barely made out the back of your truck in the tall grass," said Lisa.

"So, what do you think?" asked Earl.

"I don't know. I see amazing potential. But, it requires work that scares me to death," confessed Hannah.

Earl went to the sink and found the water to be on. "I'm surprised the water's on. So, at the least the well isn't dry. Have you checked out the heating and air unit?"

"No. Is it in the crawl space or the attic?" asked Hannah, looking for the air ducts. Then, she spotted them in the ceiling, indicating the attic.

Earl saw her gaze and knew she'd arrived at the correct conclusion, saying. "I brought a flashlight. Let's go up."

Earl confidently opened what Hannah thought was a closet, exposing a claustrophobic staircase that wound around to the attic. Lisa was smart and waited in the kitchen. They made their way up the winding stair to enter a dank attic filled with decades of dust. Earl stopped abruptly and cautioned, "Be careful. You don't know what condition these floorboards are in."

Hannah gingerly tested a board as she made her way to a monstrosity of a furnace that looked like it predated King Arthur. After giving a quick scan, she said, "It will have to go, but at least it's tied into a duct system instead of radiators, so I can add a new furnace and air conditioner."

A quick scan around the attic showed multiple nests from squirrels and an old trunk.

"What's that?" said Hannah, going straight for the trunk like the history geek she was.

"Hold on there, missy," said Earl, grabbing Hannah's arm. "I'm none too sure about these beams. Let me get the trunk and drag it by the entrance."

It took Earl a few seconds to test the boards and drag the trunk over, where they then opened it in the meager light. Inside was a mix of old pictures that seemed to span periods all the way back to the revolutionary war. There was even an old whale's tooth among the odd mix of old trinkets.

"Roots run deep around here," said Earl, looking at the photos.

"You don't think of people in rural Alabama being connected to those in the East Coast and the sea beyond, but they go all the way back to the beginning," said Hannah, marveling at the photos. She was tempted to take them, but knew they belonged to somebody and tenderly placed them back in the trunk.

After a few more comments back and forth, they made their way to the now derelict kitchen, then to the back garden to capture any remaining twilight.

Earl then announced, "We can handle it."

Lisa looked at Earl and smiled. "I know my man can do it." Lisa and Earl made the perfect couple. She knew when Earl was in the right based on his years of toil, restoring old buildings.

"You know, this plan might actually work. Hannah will get in her dream home, and I'll talk to Swanson," commented Earl.

"Great," concurred Hannah. "I've been at auctions before. There's a lot of down time waiting for the bid to end on parcels of no interest. I know there will be plenty of opportunities to approach him and make casual conversation."

Two days later, the three drove to the local high school for the auction. It was less than two blocks from home. Luckily, the signs in fields all over the county indicating the parcel numbers also screamed the date and time of the local auction. Hannah had heard contractors talking at the credit union. Apparently, the elderly patriarch of a large well-to-do family was going to a nursing home and the children needed the proceeds for his care, with money to spare for other less noble pursuits.

Hannah drove and followed the large pickups into the parking lot, trucks that carried farmers interspersed by a few sedans. While getting out of her car, Hannah noticed a local attorney and a competing bank loan officer trying to get a lead on some new business generated from the sales.

"Hey, Mike," waved Earl. "Howdy, Tom, Jim, Fred..." As usual, Earl knew everybody.

"You decided to try your hand at farming?" asked a smiling older man in a field jacket. He had the look of a successful agriculturalist who didn't care to dress up to impress others; just wore his most comfortable clothes.

"No," said Earl. "Just came with my friend here, Hannah Sparrow."

"How you doing, Mister?" asked Hannah as she extended her hand.

"Fred Griffin," he answered, shaking hands. "You're the banker. Here to do some business?"

"I'm certainly happy to take any business anybody would graciously send my way," replied Hannah as they walked toward the door. "But I also saw the house on the five-acre parcel with those trees lining the lot. I thought I'd put in a bid."

They entered what appeared to be an old gymnasium with two dozen rows of folding chairs of ten chairs each. Close to the entrance was a table with somebody taking names for bidding paddles. Hannah registered and turned in a copy of her pre-approval letter while Lisa and Earl found seats.

"Do you see Old Man Swanson?" asked Hannah, trying to scan the room without looking obvious.

"Yes," said Earl in a hushed voice. "He's over there with the two boys in the back of the room." Hannah saw a rotund older man in a sport coat looking out of place, like a gentleman farmer. You could tell by his appearance that he thought himself a cut above his neighbors. His two boys looked similar in V-neck sweaters with underlying oxford shirts like they just returned from a weekend at Cambridge. Both fingered their cell phones, apparently uninterested in who attended the proceedings.

After the crowd settled in, an auctioneer began his rapid hawking of land parcels. Hannah was amazed as men and women who she would have thought almost indigent because of their worn and patched blue jeans under barn jackets were bidding over a million dollars after checking math on their cell phones. Some had phones to their ears, conferring with family back on the farm, presumably milking cows or other tasks that couldn't be left.

When the bidding came to Hannah's little house, the auctioneer started the bidding at $15,000. Hannah held up her paddle. It appeared that there would be no other bids, until the auctioneer called everyone's attention to the fact that a purchaser could bulldoze the house and turn the five acres into prime farm land. A couple of previously disinterested farmers raised their paddles, including Swanson. The bidding rose between the three until it reached $55,000 and out of her budget. Hannah sat brooding when the house and land was awarded to Swanson. Hannah lamented the rows of carefully planted trees being plowed under by the man and his two disinterested sons who never once tore their eyes from their phones. To the positive, it provided a perfect reason for Earl to approach him.

As the bidding moved to a parcel well out of Leigh Acres, Swanson moved to a table filled with snacks and assorted refreshments. Earl saw his chance and meandered over to the table.

"Congratulations. It's a really nice house," observed Earl, retrieving a little bag of chips.

"House?" Swanson said, confused. "Oh, yes. It is a cute house. Too bad it has to go."

"Yes," confirmed Earl. "It will be a nice addition to your farm land. I believe your family goes way back in this county, don't they?"

Swanson looked at Earl with an expression like *you know I do*. So he just nodded.

"In fact, you're kin to Bobby Joe Swanson, who kept the grounds and farm for LaGrange Military Academy."

"Yes. That I am. He had two daughters. One late in life from a second marriage," he said dubiously. "I heard you were researching the old school. Some cadet's journal."

Earl was surprised. He hadn't expected their little inquiries to have made it that far up the social scale. Either that, or the families associated with LaGrange Academy were in contact with each other. He shook off the notion of a conspiracy theory.

"Two daughters you say?" continued Earl.

"Yes. Sarah was my great-grandmother," he said without elaboration.

After an uncomfortable pause as Earl hoped for more, he continued, "I understand that her sister's name was Millie. Does she have descendants around here?"

"No," he replied flatly.

"Are they somewhere else?" Earl pressed.

"Not that I know of," he said, looking away at the auctioneer.

"So, she just disappeared?"

"I know nothing about her and don't know who I would ask. I have to go," he said tersely and marched back to his seat.

Earl walked back to his seat, answering the stares of Lisa and Hannah with a downcast shrug. "So, nothing?" asked Lisa.

"Not a thing. He either doesn't know or doesn't care."

"Or, knows and doesn't want you to know," countered Hannah. "I bet that old coot knows something."

"There's always been rumors about how the family came to own half the county," added Lisa.

"What kind of rumors?" asked Hannah.

"Just vague questions more than anything. Nothing having to do with Millie that I'm aware of."

Now, Hannah was miffed. She lost her dream home to the old curmudgeon and wanted to find something. The three slipped out the back door.

In the back sat Hamady, thinking, *That woman has more lives than both her cats combined. On top of that, she obviously wants to put down even more roots. LaGrange Academy still offers the best opportunity to kill her, even if she's not roaming the cemetery. The trick is to get her there alone.*

Chapter 30
What's Next?

Hannah, Earl and Lisa sat on Hannah's porch taking stock of things now that the last interview had turned up nothing.

"There's no cadet grave at the school. We've interviewed the descendants of the doctor, headmaster, groundskeeper, and now the quartermaster. There's nobody left," recapped an exasperated Earl.

"So, what's next?" asked Lisa. "That can't be the end of it. How about the Tempest reference? I know it's mysterious, but we can work through that."

Hannah thought for a moment. "I'll call Mike at the university library. Literature is outside of my element. Maybe he has some thoughts."

Lisa looked at her with a smile. "So, you're on a first name basis?"

Hannah blushed slightly, "No we're not. Moving back to our other lines of inquiry. If Caleb, Millie, and Ridge were murdered around here, I don't think we'll find them. The only thing left is to see if they went back to Winston County or joined some Confederate unit we've not researched yet."

"But you checked the Winston area phone book for their last names and you didn't find anything. So, they don't seem to have any descendants there, which implies murder again," concluded Lisa.

"There's one place left to check: the Winston County Records Office. They record marriages and the disposition of area family members, often for property transference."

"After that, I guess I go back to the Confederate soldier archives to check military units again for those who were 'mustered out' (died) or were discharged. If discharged, they should show up in pensioner records. Soldiers who survived the war were ultimately awarded a monthly pension by the government.

"So that's it. Two more strikes and we're out," said Earl.

Hannah thought, *Let's just hope I don't get hit by a fastball in the process.*

Inevitably, Earl and Lisa went home, leaving Hannah to her little white cottage and ever-present cotton mill. In the past days, Hannah had thought she had rid herself of the feeling of fear and dread, but they were back with a vengeance. She triple-checked her locks and retreated inside, where her cats were waiting and none too happy about being locked inside.

The next day, Mike called from the library in response to Hannah's voicemail asking for help. He said he found a university professor with a background in Shakespearean plays and arranged for a meeting that same afternoon.

As a result, Hannah and Mike found themselves sitting together in Professor Janet James's office.

"You mentioned to my assistant that you're investigating a murder. I don't know how I could possibly help but, tell me what you want," commented the veteran but youthful professor with shoulder-length blond hair. Hannah felt a twinge of jealousy and suddenly regretted their new avenue of inquiry.

Hannah peered at Mike with a look that said, *I know you wanted a quick appointment, but let's see you explain "investigating a murder."*

Mike explained the journal, followed by Hannah, who walked them through the riddle.

"So, you see, the riddle ends with, '*While a Shakespearean sonnet this is not, Venture to the Tempest to find the spot.*'"

"That's intriguing," said Professor James. "*The Tempest* is a play about magic, love, and forgiveness. It's set on an island where Prospero, the former Duke of Milan, and his daughter, Miranda, live with the spirit, Ariel. Prospero creates a storm, or 'tempest,' that causes a shipwreck and creates the basis for the play. Among other things, the plot includes a romance between Miranda and the King's son, Ferdinand. In the end all the plot lines are brought together, and they all set sail for home."

"That's great," said Hannah. "Do we know where this island or 'home' are?"

"Unfortunately, no," said the professor.

"Oh," said Hannah, looking down, dejected.

"Could there be a tie to some occult or magic in the mountains?" asked Mike, looking at Hannah.

"I suppose so, but the reference to '*the spot*' seems very geographic and not mystical," she said with confusion. "It uses the word 'Venture' like a journey to a map reference. Plus, the prior sentence in the riddle reads, 'One will be buried in blue and the other in view.' The view of blue could be an island or shoreline."

"Is that just a reference to a journey?" asked Mike, thinking aloud.

"Do you have the journal with the riddle reference with you? Sometimes we can glean meaning from the exact semantics and punctuation," said the professor.

Hanna reached into a shoulder bag and retrieved the book, handing it to Dr. James, who carefully examined the journal. She started with the riddle, then scanned several other pages.

"The riddle capitalizes Venture, which would normally be lower case. In looking at the prior pages, this Caleb seems to take care to punctuate correctly. It may be that Venture is not a verb."

"So, it's not exactly referring to 'follow the yellow brick road.' It's something else," affirmed Hannah.

"Yes. Or, it could have double meaning as a noun *and* a verb. How clever and well-read do you think this cadet was?"

"He seemed very clever. He had a strong grasp of history, at least American history up to that point. He also noted his father's concern about his propensity to be found with his nose in a book."

"That's good. That increases the scope of possible meanings. Let me do some additional research to find out more," affirmed the professor gleefully. "I do love a mystery." It was then that Hannah noticed the contents of the bookshelf behind her desk. It was filled with mysteries ranging from Agatha Christie to Lillian Jackson Braun. How fortunate for Hannah.

Hannah and Mike took a few minutes to catch up on the investigation and share life's challenges in the student union. Mike mentioned that he had his share of people like old Higgins to deal with himself. After a long discussion, they both sensed that it was time to go. Any longer would clearly indicate the desire for more, and they both seemed to hesitate to take that next step.

Chapter 31
Visit the County

Hannah decided to take a couple days off and not think about the confusing note or the man who may or may not have intended to lock her in a vault. It would also give her time to cool off and not have to see old Clyde.

She approached the Winston County Courthouse. She'd been to quite a few county facilities in various states, researching land records, especially during her time at the Bureau of Indian Affairs. She always chuckled at how they all had the same look and personality. They were always constructed of gray stone with thick walls and, often, had bars on the windows. Just walking in gave you a feeling of deep foreboding. Even the air seemed centuries old. Daylight dwindled as you entered corridors with little signs painted on glass doors or protruding from the upper reach of the door jamb on a piece of wood.

Hannah made her way inside and found that they had the sign protruding from the door jamb models. She made her way to the door marked "marriage licenses." That normally meant the records room.

Inside, Hannah lamented that it would have been nice to be seeking a marriage license rather than looking for dead people. She nevertheless approached the counter that was devoid of requesters. A woman of sixty rose from her desk and flashed Hannah a smile. "How can I help you?"

"I was doing some genealogy research and was hoping to find these three names from around the time of the Civil War." Hannah handed over the three names.

The woman said, "Normally we charge an hourly research fee and ask that you leave the names for a week."

"Oh," said Hannah, disappointed. "I'm fine with a research fee. Is there any way to pay express charges?"

Looking around, the lady announced, "You're in luck. My daughter called and said she'd be late in picking me up for lunch. So, I have some extra time. Let me look at our cross-reference system."

Hannah leaned on the counter while she looked up some records. "I found a reference to Caleb Rochester. It records him as the son of Emory Rochester. But I don't see anything regarding a marriage or death. It seems that the property was transferred to an elder brother Douglas. From the looks of it, it's been rezoned into an agricultural parcel and sold off to a corporate farm. The house may be there in ruins, but is more likely plowed under a field. I don't have a physical address since there is none, but here's the general location and an original surveyor's drawing. I know there's an old general store, if you can call it that, right near there. The owner, Old Man Willard, is always there, usually on the front porch. He can direct you a little closer—here's the address."

About that time, a woman entered who had the same facial features as the mother, indicating that it was time to go.

"So, that's it," said Hannah.

"I'm sorry. Leave your number. If I find anything else, I'll call you."

Hannah thanked her and drove out to the homestead.

She located the address of what she expected to be a Normal Rockwell type of store typically seen on a postcard. This one looked like a cross between a secondhand store and a car accident.

But, there was a porch and on it an old man wearing bib overalls and a flannel shirt, despite the summer heat. Hannah approached him and said, "Muriel at the County Records Office said you might direct me to this old homestead."

"Well, did she now?" he said, reaching for the paper. Glancing at it, he said, "I know where this is. I used to play in the old shack as a kid. Part of it is still there inside the rows of corn."

"Can you write the directions?"

"Yes, I can. While I do that, you might do me a favor and see if there's anything inside that you'd like to purchase." His request was friendly but direct, as in "I'll scratch your back if you scratch mine and buy something."

Hannah thought back to when she last received a tetanus shot and entered. Aside from its outward appearance as a dump, the inside indicated that it was a dump and a half. However, there were sporadic items of interest claiming her attention, like a pair of twisted candlesticks made to look like snakes. There was a teapot fashioned like a frog, with the tea poured from its open mouth. There were also old uniforms from both the Union and the Confederacy in equal proportion. Hannah chose the frog teapot, wondering if he would wrap it in tissue, or a rat's nest from behind the counter.

Hannah walked out with the frog tea set. "How much for this?"

"Well, that was a prized possession of my dear grandmother. Let me think for a second," said the cunning old coot. "I'll give it to you for $20. I'll take cash or a debit card."

She was going to pay in cash but decided to use a debit card just to see what he'd do with it. He took the card and went inside, where he cleared a space on the counter by removing what appeared to be a stuffed beaver. He reached under a shelf and retrieved what Hannah recognized as a state-of-the-art processing machine linked to a laptop computer. He saw her expression and said, "I would also have accepted PayPal, Cube, Popmoney, and any card excluding Discover."

While he wrapped Hannah's teapot in bubble wrap he'd retrieved from an Amazon box, she asked about the uniforms. "I was surprised to see Yankee and Confederate uniforms together. I'd have thought that you'd only find old Confederate uniforms around here."

"In this county, we had almost as many folks go north to fight for the Union as the Confederacy." That pronouncement hit Hannah like a ton of bricks. Maybe she had been searching the wrong military records.

"Really?" she blurted.

"Yes, really. The 1st Alabama Cavalry was raised mainly from farmers around here that gathered in Huntsville to go north. It was attached to the XVI Corps and mainly did scouting and reconnaissance because they knew the South so well. They also flanked the infantry while on the march to guard against Confederate attacks."

"I had no idea," said Hannah. "What became of them?"

"I believe their last major assignment was escorting General Sherman as his personal bodyguard during his march to the sea. But, if you're asking if many died, the answer is yes. They lost about four hundred of their number out of almost two thousand, not all from Alabama. Those poor fellers died fighting in quite a few battles including Monroe's Crossroads and Bentonville.

They were even there for the surrender of the Confederate Army of Tennessee."

"Why do you say poor fellers? Because of the depravation and horrors of war?" asked Hannah.

"Not just that. Winston County folks was sufferin' from their own internal war. The Confederate Home Guards in the county used their uniforms as an excuse to punish those families they suspected had a family member fighting for the Union. These families responded by forming their own unofficial home guard to fight back. By the end of the war, Winston County was devastated by its own kind."

"Is that what happened to the Rochester homestead?" asked Hannah.

"I don't know that name, but that's not surprising. Many folks left the area after the troubles. Even after the war, Winston County was at odds with the rest of Alabama. This county had a goodly number of Republicans, which was more like Democrats today that pushed for more federal power to fund projects like the railroad and curb state's rights. The rest of the state was made of Democrats, like Republicans today, that opposed federal government expansion and social issues. Did you have a chance to see the Dual Destiny statue when you were downtown?"

"No, why? What is it?" asked Hannah.

"It's a statue of a soldier dressed half Union in blue and half Confederate in gray."

Hannah thanked the man and drove in a daze to the old homestead. The chimney from the fireplace rose from the corn like an alien marker left by an unknown host. Hannah looked at the brick and spoke to it, saying, "Where did your family go? Did Ridge die at the school, or join the Union army? Did his family get killed by the Confederate Home Guard? Or, did they come home to you after the war? If they did, why aren't there any records of them? Why won't you tell me?"

Hanna's phone rang, which made her jump. She composed herself and replied sheepishly, as if not wanting a bullet to come through the phone. "Hello. This is Hannah."

"Hello, Hannah. This is Professor James. I think I found the answer to the last part of your riddle. Or at least I've narrowed down the area."

Hanna breathed a sigh of relief. "Hi, professor. That's welcome news. What did you find?"

"I reread *The Tempest* and found nothing. Then, I consulted with a maritime history professor and found that 'Venture' is both a noun and a verb in this instance. It turns out that William Shakespeare was inspired to write *The Tempest* based on a real event involving a ship of that name."

"Wow," exclaimed Hanna. "Please, tell me more."

"Basically, a fleet of almost a dozen ships sailed from England with provisions and settlers on route to what's now known as the Jamestown Colony of Virginia. Unfortunately, a storm separated one of the ships, the *Sea Venture*, which wrecked on the uninhabited island of Bermuda. The surviving crew miraculously built two boats and continued on their way across the ocean to Jamestown. Incidentally, one of the crewmen never left the island and became its first settler. When they returned to England, their story became big news and apparently inspired William Shakespeare to write *The Tempest*."

"So, the destination is either Jamestown, Bermuda, or the UK?" conjectured Hannah.

"I think it's clearly Bermuda," concluded the professor. "Technically, *Venture* never made it to Jamestown or England. It wrecked at Bermuda."

"How big is Bermuda?"

"I looked-it up on a map. It's only about ten miles long."

"I vaguely recall that Caleb had a great uncle that settled in Bermuda after being on a merchant ship," mused Hannah aloud.

"So, Caleb may have been familiar with the story," responded the professor. "That's a possible link."

Hannah looked around, trying to replace the scenery with the ocean surrounding Bermuda. Then, she thought despondently, *If I can't find answers here, how could I even begin to look for them in a foreign country? I'm not exactly Interpol.*

Hannah proceeded home. On the way, she'd call Mike at the university. Maybe he could get his friends at the national archives to research the Alabama Cavalry that fought for the Union. It was a longshot, but maybe Caleb and Ridge had switched sides.

Chapter 32
Unknown Caller

Hannah spent a fitful night despite knowing that Earl, Houdini and Sugar Ray were doing their nightly rounds of her house. She needed caffeine and decided to go to the garage convenience store. She was in a sour mood and had no interest in talking to the owner, so she decided to fill up and pay at the pump, followed by using the vending machine out front typically for after-hours purchases. But, as she emerged from her car, he walked out of the garage.

"Do you want regular unleaded?"

Hannah said, "Yes, please. But here's my card."

"Don't worry about it. I got this. That's one benefit of owning the place. When you drove up, you looked a little down."

As he pumped the gas, Hannah said, "I don't really know your name."

"It's Dusty Morris, Hannah."

"Should I be flattered?" she said with a seductive smile.

He pointed to her credit union security badge on her dashboard with "Hannah" emblazoned under her picture.

"Oh," she said sheepishly. "That's also how you knew I worked at the credit union at my last visit. I was wearing my badge."

"Don't feel embarrassed. I asked my guys if they knew you and they said no." At Dusty's mention of the "guys," he and Hannah looked over at the garage, where they saw three guys watching the spectacle. In response, the guys quickly turned and pretended they were doing something mechanical.

Dusty finished pumping the gas and said, "Hey, maybe you'd like to get..." He paused in thought.

"Let me guess, knowing my terrible eating habits, you can't think of what we'd get at a real restaurant?" laughed Hannah.

"Something like that," Dusty said. "Given more time, I'll think of something not involving anything healthy."

"I'm fine with healthy as long as it's deep fried," chuckled Hannah at her own joke. Then, she added, "I'd love to go wherever you choose. Next time I'm here getting bologna, we can decide when and where. Or, you can give me your number."

"It's a date."

Hannah was about to turn into her driveway when she got a text signed by Earl indicating that he found something and needed to see Hannah at LaGrange Military Academy. Hannah smiled thinking that Earl was getting into the twentieth century and started texting. She never thought to look at the number because Earl had a flip phone and she assumed he probably borrowed a smartphone from a coworker.

It was getting dark when Hannah arrived on the mountain. She grabbed her B-Lite in case they needed to look at something in the old ruin. She learned to carry the heavy flashlight, about a foot long and made of etched metal making it more lethal than a billy club when checking building sites at night.

Hannah had a strange feeling and proceeded cautiously onto the grounds. Like an old barnyard, there was only one overhead light on a pole, giving the faintest illumination. From her training, Hannah automatically stayed out of the light and skirted its edges as she looked for her neighbor.

"Earl!" Hannah shouted several times.

Earl wasn't in sight. Then, Hannah saw the darting light of another flashlight in the old ruins and went inside.

"Earl!" she said again. The flashlight illumination had gone. Knowing that any reasonable person would have returned her hails to make themselves known, Hannah slowly backed away to return to the outside. Then, in a frozen second, she saw a shadow come at her from the corner of her eye. Instinctively, she swung her B-Lite in the direction of the movement and connected just as she was likewise hit in the head, followed by searing pain. Hannah staggered and tried to keep conscious as she half ran, half crawled outside. Dazed, Hannah saw headlights near the entrance. In her confusion, she debated calling for help, fearing that the vehicle's driver was with his attacker.

Then, she saw the truck skid to a stop and the driver emerged yelling, "Hey, you there, stop!"

Hannah could sense that a very small man or woman was running away into the darkness. The driver emerged next to Hannah. "Earl?" she asked.

"No, it's Mike, from the University Library."

"Did you see who hit me?" said Hannah, now sitting down, trying to focus.

"No. I couldn't see them," said Mike. "We've got to get you to a hospital."

"I'm okay," argued Hannah. "How did you know to come here?"

"I got some information from the military archives and tried calling you but didn't get you. Since I was curious to see the school after your description anyway, I drove here."

"Yes, it's sometimes hard to get cell coverage here in the country," she said, holding her head.

"I'm taking you to the hospital. A blow to the head is nothing to fool with. You're not thinking straight," said Mike, getting Hannah to her feet.

Then everything went black.

Hannah woke up in the hospital to an empty room. Her head was sore, and somebody was trying to kill her. Things couldn't get any worse, or could they?

"It serves you right," said Clyde Higgins after barging in.

"Serves me right? Having somebody try to kill me?"

"That's right. You brought it on yourself," said Higgins, shaking his finger in Hannah's face.

But Hannah's eyes focused on the two men who slipped in behind him. Mike from the university and Dick McKenna, the credit union president.

"Mr. Higgins. It's time for you to go," said McKenna.

"But I'm just protecting the credit union," objected Higgins.

"We don't need your protection. It appears that Hannah needs protection from you. So, like I said, it's time for you to go," said McKenna again.

"Okay. I'll go and talk to you about it tomorrow."

"You don't understand," said McKenna. "It's time for you to go from the credit union. You're fired. Now, get out before I have you removed."

Higgins tried to protest but McKenna interjected. "As you know, I'm on the hospital board and have no problem having security remove you."

Higgins left in a huff saying, "You'll be sorry."

Then, McKenna turned to Mike and said, "Thanks for calling me. I had no idea he was so out of control. And, as for you, Miss Sparrow, just focus on getting well. Your job, or should I say, Higgins's job, will be waiting for you." As quickly as McKenna appeared, he left, leaving Mike.

"You called him?" asked Hannah.

"Mr. McKenna is also on the university's library board. I called to tell him you were here. I guess I may have also mentioned your struggles with old Higgins relative to keeping the bank square with the regulators."

"Are you feeling better?" asked Mike.

"Okay, I guess. How long have I been in here?"

"Just overnight. Lisa and Earl are here too. I saw that they were recent callers on your phone and took a chance. They went to get us some food from the cafeteria. The doctor says you have a concussion but should be okay.

"When you called the numbers on the phone, did you happen to reach who sent the text?"

"Nobody answered that one. I assume they used a disposable phone that can't be traced. I contacted the police to investigate."

Then, Hannah remembered the reason for his visit on the mountain. "You said your sources found something in the Union archives?"

"You sure you want to think about that right now?" Mike asked with a look of concern.

"I seem to have nothing else to do and certainly nowhere to go," commented Hannah, pointing at her hospital gown, conspicuously tied in the back.

"Well, my friends at the national center looked into the First Alabama Cavalry that accompanied Sherman on his march to the sea. There was one with the name Ridge. Apparently, it was a common name, like John or Bob would be today. Names seem to come and go in popularity over time. However, there weren't any with the last names Sexton or Rochester. I printed some lists that you can take home and review if you'd like. I also did more research into ties between Southerners and Sherman to look for clues, but nothing concrete emerged."

Hannah tried to hide her disappointment. "It was so gracious of you to do this and bring the results for me to look at. And, I don't think I ever thanked you for saving me."

"I don't know that I saved you—I just happened to get there and spook the robber, or whatever they were."

"By the way," said Hannah, trying to brighten the subject. "Professor James called. She figured out the *Tempest* reference." Hannah summarized her findings to a clearly captivated Mike.

"So, we have two broad locations to examine," concluded Mike.

"What's the second exactly?" asked a confused Hannah.

"The second has to do with Sherman's march to the sea. The southern boys knew the terrain and acted as scouts for Sherman's army. They were even said to be his personal bodyguard in his travels—including his visit to his love interest in Georgia," continued Mike.

"The march to the sea went through two or three states. That's a lot of areas to look for clues," observed Hannah.

"I know, but that's all I've got," said Mike with a shrug.

Hannah decided to move the subject in a more personal, different direction. "How did Sherman find the love of his life in Georgia? He was fighting for his life for heaven's sake—not unlike myself of late."

"When Sherman attended West Point, he had a roommate from Georgia whose sister visited to attend an academy dance. When their eyes met, Sherman fell in love. Unfortunately, she found his eyes less endearing and is said to have commented, 'Your eyes are so cold and cruel. I pity the man who ever becomes your foe. Ah, how you would crush an enemy.' To this,

Sherman replied, 'Even though you were my enemy, my dear, I would ever love and protect you,'" said Mike with a dramatic flourish.

"So, did he?" asked Hannah.

"No, despite saving her home from destruction on his march to the sea, he never saw her after the dance."

"How sad," said Hannah, staring into Mike's eyes. "He certainly never forgot her."

"Seeing your eyes, I understand his reaction," said Mike, moving closer.

Then, the doctor came in, wrecking the perfect moment. Lisa and Earl returned about that time with the Leigh Acres police chief in tow to take Hannah's statement. He was short, with a crew cut and black cargo pants that seemed to display the bravado of a SWAT team that the town didn't have.

"So, there was nothing taken and you were summoned there by somebody claiming they were Earl," he said incredulously. "Tell me again why you thought it was Earl when he's never texted you before."

Hannah described the journal and their investigation into what had happened to the cadet.

The police chief just shook his head. "I can't see why anybody would want to hurt you over some history hobby. Are you sure you're telling me everything?"

Hannah looked at Lisa, then Earl, then Mike to see if she had left anything out. "That's everything."

"Regarding the vault, are you sure it wasn't simply a thoughtful citizen who saw the light and closed the vault door to protect its contents after hours?" continued the chief.

"Surely the two incidents can't be a coincidence," said Lisa irritably.

"Under the circumstances, it's not unusual for people to think they heard or saw something that wasn't there and I believe this to be a robbery attempt and the other just an accident," said the chief as nicely as he could. Then before anybody would object further he added, "But, we'll treat it as a threat and schedule extra patrols around Ms. Sparrow's house."

Hannah cut off the group from further protests by saying, "Thank you, Chief. That's very gracious of you."

"I'll write this up and you can swing by the station tomorrow to sign." With that, he departed, leaving the four to commiserate.

"I can't believe after all that, he thinks it's a simple case of robbery," said Lisa.

"I know you three have raised some local eyebrows with your inquiries, but I don't see anything that would warrant an attack, even if the cadets were murdered 150 years ago," commented Mike. "Could it actually be a robbery attempt?"

"I suppose the only way it could be caused by the investigation is if it was bigger than we thought. Like there was a mass murder of the whole squad of cadets by the others. Or, several died at the hands of a doctor doing a medical experiment with his home brew," said Hannah.

"Don't forget, we have the quartermaster and accomplices stealing from the school. They might have continued to cheat the Confederate Army. That might be worth hurting you to stop that from coming out," mused Lisa.

They continued to discuss it until Hannah was discharged. Lisa drove her home while Mike and Earl went to retrieve the truck.

"So, what do you think about Mike?" asked Lisa.

"Do you mean, could he be involved in the attack? Or, the other thing?" asked Hannah.

"No, the other thing. He seems cute and he stayed around all night to make sure you were okay. I can't see him being with the attacker; he's too new here and seems to have no connection in any way."

"I suppose you're right. Anyway, he seems too cute to be a bad guy, but I've been wrong before," lamented Hannah.

"You and me both, sister," answered Lisa with a laugh.

When they got home, the cats were waiting in the window and expressed their displeasure of having to miss a couple of meals. Hannah admonished them for not noticing her bandage and fed them. While they were eating, Hannah prepared for bed and told them, "The police will be doing extra patrols. So, don't be afraid if you see car lights swing by." Then she thought, *At least the car lights from drug dealers are being replaced by police cars. That's one small benefit.* She went to bed.

Chapter 33
Trouble at the Mill

Hannah spent the next two days on the hammock recuperating. Earl and Lisa brought over healthy food and Mike called to check on her a couple times. Except for the healthy food, she thought things were pretty cushy. Her horrible boss was gone. The chief followed through on his word and a patrol car slowed in front of her house a few times. But, the fact remained that somebody had tried to kill her. It was hard to compensate for that.

Hannah dozed in the hammock again after a fitful sleep the night before. Her mother always said that Hannah could fall asleep running for a bus, and it was true. She awoke in the twilight of approaching evening. The green sculpted lawn that Hannah and Earl had tamed now started to turn slightly brown with the heat. Hannah watched lazily as the sun fell, leaving darkness and eerie shadows.

Then, an eerie glow barely showed through the half-broken windows of the cotton mill. Hannah watched as it was quickly replaced by beams of light spastically moving from wall to wall. *But why?* wondered Hannah. *There's really nothing of value to steal.* At a loss, Hannah grabbed her smartphone and rang up Lisa and Earl. Earl answered with his flip phone, having no desire to move to the new technology.

"Hi, Hannah. Everything okay?" asked Earl.

"Hannah replied, "Someone's poking around the old mill with a flashlight. Should I be concerned?"

Earl paused to ponder the situation. "I suppose not. If it was the old dry goods store, I'd expect they'd be thieving. But round the cotton mill, I expect it's the local police after your report."

"I suppose it's nothing," said Hannah ruefully. "Probably just the police or kids looking around on a dare."

"I'll check it out with you if you want," offered Earl.

"No, I'll bet it's nothing. I guess I'll see you tomorrow. Thanks, Earl," said Hannah, hanging up.

Hannah turned her attention to a couple dishes in the kitchen at the back of the little house. Hannah had never invested in a dishwasher given that she typically used paper plates for deli carry-out. She returned to the living room and noticed that the flashlight had ceased, but was replaced by a wild glow with dancing images on the windows. Then it hit her. "Fire!"

Hannah called 911. She tried to explain that there was a fire at the old cotton mill in Leigh Acres. The operator asked her the address of the mill.

"I don't think it even has an address," she said, frustrated.

"What's the name of the mill?" the operator asked.

"It's just the old mill in Leigh Acres," answered Hannah, now exasperated. "Leigh Acres is only two blocks long in any direction. Just look for the only building in town that's on fire!"

A short ten minutes later, there was life at the volunteer fire department just a block away. It started with one member in Hannah's same block running to the station after apparently receiving the call. Then, two pickup trucks came to a screeching halt in front of the station. Just moments after that, the large door rose and the fire truck came the one block to the cotton mill.

They hooked up one hose as other cars and trucks began to arrive with a second hose added. Within minutes, the fire was out. Hannah held the cats, who watched all the action with suspicion from inside the house. Unfortunately, an upper skylight was destroyed to vent the heat out of the building to lessen the spread of fire or an explosion. But the picturesque nature of the building survived for future photographers.

The police and fire chiefs came to Hannah's house together.

"We're here for another statement," the police chief announced. That's twice now," he said seriously.

Hannah took the inference to mean you're the only common thread and automatically a suspect of the fire *and* possibly staging an attack on yourself. So Hannah replied, "Well, I certainly couldn't give myself a concussion and have a UNA professor see a fleeing suspect if I did that one myself. And, I wouldn't call the fire department if I wanted to see the building across the street burn, would I?"

"I didn't mean to imply anything, I'm just saying it," said the chief without any humor or apology in his voice. It was obvious that he had his suspicions.

The fire chief asked if Hannah saw anybody fleeing the scene. She said no.

He then mentioned, "Typically, arsonists remain behind to watch the fire. But you were the only person viewing the fire that we know of."

"That's because I'm the only one living by the building," Hannah said indignantly.

There was no response.

They left and Hannah felt slightly violated, thinking, *They should thank me for making the call and saving the building instead of making me a suspect. I need to figure out who's doing this to me.*

Earl and Lisa walked over after talking to a volunteer firefighter they knew. They didn't have anything new to share, just Earl's conclusion: "I don't see that this is related to our investigation."

"Unless the evidence we're seeking is closer to home?" conjectured Lisa.

Then Earl said, "We have to bring this to an end. Let's go through the cotton mill and the abandoned dry goods store tomorrow and look for something, anything. They're so close together that they're practically joined. So, maybe the arsonist thought that the cotton mill being more combustible would quickly spread and destroy the other building as well."

"So, the fire was meant to hide something?" asked Hannah. "But what?"

"I don't know," shrugged Earl. "But that's about all I can think of."

Chapter 34
Hamady

Hannah promised Earl and Lisa that she'd wait for one of them before searching the buildings. So, as soon as Lisa got home the next day, the two decided to enter the old dry goods store first. Earl was detained a little longer and was going to follow. The back door was unlocked, which was unusual. Everyone knew that the dry goods store contained old items still in their original packaging. People commented often that somebody should notify the producers of a TV show that specialized in going through junk. They would have a field day shopping in a store that was neatly organized with the antiques still in the box, ready for sale. Everyone wondered why Hamady never sold the place and its contents, figuring that he probably didn't need the money.

"Amazing, isn't it?" commented Lisa "I remember coming here as a kid. My dad would buy me some candy to take to the old theater up the street because it was cheaper here."

"I guess some things never change," confirmed Hannah. "I stop at the gas station to buy my popcorn on the way, too."

"That doesn't really count," said Lisa, shaking her head. "You buy *all* your meals at the gas station."

"True," confessed Hannah.

"There was a rumor that Great Grandad Hamady had a secret room upstairs where he perfected his home brew. It was said to pass down from generation to generation."

"Would people still be buying moonshine now that prohibition has gone away?" asked a confused Hannah.

"No, but dealers are dealers, and there's money to be made in anything from drugs to sex. Let's start looking upstairs," said Lisa, moving toward the wide staircase in the middle of the store. The edges of the wood were well worn from a century of shoes descending the steps. Each step by Hannah and Lisa created what seemed like an ear-splitting squeak. They reached the top and found a bunch of toys: baseballs and bats, dolls, wooden horses, and more.

"The toys were too expensive for most people back in the day. So, they eventually migrated upstairs to be stored until the next Christmas," observed Lisa.

"So, what did they do for toys?" asked Hannah.

"Well, I had cousins on the farm that made a ball out of a sheep's bladder," said Lisa.

Then, Hannah noticed two coffins stacked horizontally in the corner. In the dim light, she first took them for a large counter.

"Coffins?" observed Hannah

"Yes. In the old days, people came here for that too. They bought the casket and took it home."

"It's convenient that two coffins are so close by," said Hamady in a guttural tone

"Oh, Mr. Hamady. I hope you don't mind us coming here. We were just trying to figure out why somebody would want to burn the cotton mill. We thought maybe there was a connection here somewhere." It was then that they saw the .357 Magnum and a gas can in his hand.

"I don't understand," said Hannah.

"What's to understand? You're getting too close and costing me too much money," said Hamady.

"Why is our investigation of the academy costing you money?" asked Hannah.

"What? I don't care about some academy. It all started when you cut the grass," said Hamady, waving the gun that looked half his size.

"Come again?" said Lisa, seeming unafraid due to the snide inflection in her question. Even while facing a .357 Magnum, she still had "attitude."

"Yes, the grass. My customers moved down the road to a drug dealer in Town Creek because you exposed where they meet me to buy drugs outside my lab and sometimes an occasional high school girl recruited for an evening's fun. Before you moved in, it was perfect. The Leigh Acres police never went on night patrol because they don't have the staff. The county sheriff keeps his patrols to the county roads, and people would never think to report something suspicious only a block from the Police Station. They assumed nobody would be that bold. But you bought the place from the senile old lady who slept her life away. Unlike her, you're always looking out the window. To make matters worse, you cut the grass and exposed our little business. My customers got scared off along with the toadies I used to recruit the girls."

"I'm sorry. I can let the grass grow again," offered Hannah feebly.

"It's a little late for that, don't you think? I tried to warn you. I repainted gang symbols to keep you away. Then, I tried to scare you into moving by vandalizing your home and poisoning your cat. I wrote you a note. I even killed those useless old sisters from the mountains that talked to you at the church. Then, I tried to kill you—twice. The only thing left was burning the old mill."

"You killed those old women? Why? They didn't tell me anything," objected Hannah.

"I couldn't take that chance," he said with a shrug.

Hannah stood silent in shock.

Lisa took up the questioning to try and keep Hamady talking. "Why would you want to burn the old mill? Wouldn't that have burned this building too?"

"No. This old store building is solid brick—and just down from the firehouse. They'd have hosed down this building and kept the cotton mill from spreading. The metal frame of the cotton mill and its structure would have survived."

"I still don't understand how that would have helped the drug business," said Hannah, now coming around.

Hamady clenched his free fist even more. "Don't you see? An ugly eyesore across from you would have finally driven you away, or at least convinced you to let the tall grass grow to cover the view. Then my customers would return."

"Oh," was all Hannah could think to say while she searched for anything to buy more time.

"Now, I can burn the mill and your bodies together. I'll make it look like you started the fire in a misguided attempt to beautify the neighborhood. Then, we go back to the way things were. My drugs can start flowing again."

Hannah gave Lisa a sideways glance that continued to some baseball bats nearby. "But I didn't know you meant 'stop cutting the grass' when your note said to put things back to the way they were. And, where it said to 'mind my business,' I didn't know you were referring to looking out the window. You really should have been more descriptive in your letter. I thought you were talking about LaGrange Academy," said Hannah defensively.

"Do you really think this is a good time to critique the man's writing?" asked Lisa, playing along to keep him distracted.

"I'm just saying..." said Hannah.

"Shut up, both of you!" yelled Hamady.

"You know, you haven't really committed any crime in front of us. We'll just forget this whole thing," said

Hannah like it was a done deal and started down the steps.

Hannah didn't realistically think that he would be persuaded by such a lame argument. But she needed to draw his attention away from Lisa, who grabbed a bat and threw it at Hamady. Miraculously, it hit Hamady in the temple and left him temporarily stunned. With that, both women flew down the stairs and dodged the ensuing bullets as they dove behind shelves in two different directions. Luckily, Lisa had the presence of mind to head straight for the electrical box, where she yanked out the breakers, leaving them all in relative darkness due to boarded-up windows.

Hannah tried to crouch as best she could, slowing her breathing to a crawl despite being out of breath from the exertion and excitement.

"You two can't hide forever," said Hamady.

But Lisa and Hannah both knew that they didn't have to hide forever. Leigh Acres was only a couple blocks long. The gunshots had to be heard by somebody. In the country, the sounds of sport use were easy to identify with the slow, methodical firing at targets. These shots were rapid, like a violent gunfight.

Hannah heard Hamady breathing just a few inches away and fought the urge to attack him or flee. It was almost pitch black where she crouched and he would pass by if Hannah was careful.

Then, they heard movement in another corner of the store; so did the gunman, who went in that direction. It was too late; Earl was on him like a "hobo on a ham sandwich." In a split second, Earl slammed him to the ground and kneeled on his back. He didn't have to kneel long because the police chief had heard the shots at home, just a block away, and pushed his way through the back door as Lisa turned on the lights. It was a lucky thing too, because Hannah was about to pounce, saying, "I'll show you to hurt my cat and those harmless old ladies."

"It's okay, Chief. It's Earl," Earl said, raising his hands. Having Earl know everybody in town came in handy at times like this.

"Stop them!" yelled Hamady. "They were robbing the dry goods store and I caught them. Then, they pulled a gun."

The chief looked at Earl, followed by a glance at Lisa and Hannah. He retrieved his handcuffs from his gun belt and secured Hamady's wrists. He and Earl raised the still protesting man, who finally fell silent as the chief showed he wasn't buying it and began to read him his rights, saying, "You have the right to remain silent, you have the right to…"

It took over two hours at the Police Station for Hannah, Lisa, and Earl to tell the story. The complication wasn't so much about the dry goods store arrest. It was explaining the LaGrange Military Academy investigation to a small gallery of officers and residents who came to hear the news.

Finally, the chief said, "So it was never about your investigation. It was always about drugs. Cutting the grass triggered this whole event."

"I guess so" was all Hannah could say.

"We suspected Hamady of dealing drugs but never thought he'd do it right by the station under our noses. This will be a good opportunity to go back to the town board and petition to replace the funds in our budget to put night patrols back on permanently. That way, nobody will ever follow Hamady's lead."

With that, Hannah, Earl, and Lisa walked the block from the corrugated building that served as City Hall, the Police Station, the Water Department, the Land Office, and a few other city functions. This was one of those occasions that having everything in Leigh Acres within two blocks was convenient.

"So, what about Caleb, Ridge, and Millie?" asked Earl, disappointed.

"I guess we'll never know," said Hannah.

"So that's it?" asked Lisa.

"I have a couple vacation days left. If you watch Lilly and Baxter, I think I'll take a little trip to the Etowah River."

"Why there?" asked Lisa.

"It's something Mike said at the hospital. He mentioned some Alabama boys from the First Alabama Cavalry rode with Sherman on his march to the sea, which included a stop-off at the house of a lady friend. I did some research on my smartphone and found that the home is only a few hours from here and supposed to be magnificent. It's a thin lead, but maybe somebody there knows who the boys in the bodyguard were. A couple from Winston county may have even stayed because they couldn't go home."

"But I thought that Mike didn't find Caleb or Ridge in the roster for the First Alabama Cavalry. How could they be in the bodyguard?"

"He did find Ridge with a different last name. I found that some boys changed their name for various reasons when they joined. Some girls did too, for obvious reasons. I know it's a long shot, but I can't find them here or in their home county. So, it's my way of refusing to acknowledge they're in an unmarked grave somewhere," said Hannah, trying to sound convincing.

"I think the trip might do her good," said Earl with a smile. "If this doesn't pan out, we'll still be here to help any way we can."

Chapter 35
The Rest of the Story

Hannah drove through several small towns until she finally reached the Etowah River and saw the house on the bluff. She made her way through a winding road halfway up the hill when she saw a Victorian-era bed and breakfast with a hand-chiseled wooden sign that read, "Poor Richard's Inn. Owned by the Franklin Family since 1867." In between the "Poor Richard's Inn" and "Owned by the Franklin Family" was a key descending from the heavens on a lightning bolt.

She slowed in front of the sign and thought, *Benjamin Franklin unlocked the secret of lightning when he used a kite and a key in his experiment. He also wrote under the pseudonym Poor Richard when writing his almanac. What does that have to do with Caleb and Ridge?* Then it hit her: *They were referring to his friend, John Paul, in the riddle. I had the wrong Paul the whole time!*

That was it. The riddle made it so clear the whole time. Why didn't she see it? She rolled into the parking lot, went inside, and requested a room. A kindly husband and wife behind a Civil War-era wood counter reached behind to a cabinet containing several cubby holes corresponding to different bedrooms.

"You've been here since the Civil War, I see," observed Hannah.

"That's right," replied the older man. "My great-grandfather came here during the war and fell in love with the area."

"Let me guess. His name was Ridge or Caleb," she said, smiling.

"That's right. It was Ridge. How did you know?"

"He was mentioned in a diary at LaGrange Military Academy."

By now, his wife appeared at his side.

Hannah explained her finding the journal. How she, Earl, and Lisa tried to solve the riddle and mistakenly thought it referred to Paul in the Bible.

"So," explained Hannah, "when I saw 'Poor Richard's Inn and the Franklin Family,' it hit me like a lightning bolt."

She wrote down the riddle, so they could see it, and pointed at each phrase to explain.

Like Paul who fled from murder a deed he did, to meet a man who unlocked a heaven's light hid,

But enemies would follow him ashore, as a crown pursued a good man the more,

So, Caleb and Ridge did the same, to reach an end with poor Richard's name.

One will be buried in blue and the other in view.

While a Shakespearean sonnet this is not, Venture to the Tempest to find the spot.

"Ridge's friend had a grandfather who was a Continental soldier and an uncle who had met John Paul Jones. He said so in his friend's journal, but it didn't occur to me at the time that the poem was about John Paul. That was his real name. The surname, Jones, was added after a murder to disguise his identity."

"What murder?" asked the old man.

"When John Paul (before he added Jones to his name) was captain of a British ship, he had a man disciplined by having him subjected to several lashes, which was the standard practice of the time. But, the man died. The victim was well connected and John Paul was accused of murder. It turned out that the man was suffering from yellow fever, which wasn't taken into account at his death. Fearing that he would be convicted by a court stacked with people from the influential family, John Paul fled to America and changed his name to John Jones. Once here, Jones met and became friends with Benjamin Franklin," explained Hannah.

The old man interjected, "Benjamin Franklin who flew a kite in attempt to have it hit by lightning. He had a line tied to a key, which was to collect the electricity traveling down the line where Franklin would drop it into a jar. In the process, he discovered electricity in lightning, 'unlocking heaven's light.'"

"That's correct," said Hannah. "Then, Jones obtained a contract with the Continental Congress to put his skills as a ship captain to use on board an armed merchantman harassing the British supply lines, which took him all the way to Great Britain. So, 'But enemies would follow him ashore, as a crown pursued a good man the more,' refers to his famous battle where the British warship, *Serapis,* pursued Jones and his ship, the *Bone Homme Richard,* where they had their famous fight."

"The one where the British captain asked him to surrender and he replied, 'I have not yet begun to fight,'" said the old man's wife.

"Right again," said Hannah. "When Jones got his command, he named the ship in honor of his friend Benjamin Franklin's famous publication, *Good Man Richard's Almanac.* The name, Bonne Home Richard, in French is 'Good Man Richard.' So, the second part of that phrase in the riddle, 'as a crown pursued a good man the more,' refers to his ship. Caleb took care to write in his journal that his great-uncle knew John Paul

Jones, who had imparted his reason for escaping to America."

Hannah continued: "The next part of the riddle reads, 'So, Caleb and Ridge did the same, to reach an end with poor Richard's name.'"

"That's where Franklin comes in," said the old man.

"Yes, Poor Richard was the pen name of Benjamin Franklin. So, in other words, Poor Richard's name is 'Franklin' in the riddle. The interesting part is the beginning of the next line. If we read that in its entirety, it says, 'So, Caleb and Ridge did the same, to reach an end with poor Richard's name.' I found the 'with' confusing at first. You'd normally say 'in' somebody's name. So, Caleb was saying he and his best friend Ridge took the name, not that he did something in somebody's name."

"In short, Caleb and Ridge did the same as John Paul Jones. John Paul changed his last name to Jones when going to America to fight for the fledging union. Caleb and Ridge changed their last names to Franklin. Ridge switched sides and fought for the union under an assumed name to protect his family."

"We knew that Great-Granddad changed the name to Franklin to protect the family back home," said the old man. "But he never mentioned a riddle. So, I guess it worked, because you couldn't find his name when researching his regiment."

"You're right. A friend examined the list of soldiers in the First Alabama Cavalry, and he found the first name, Ridge, with a different last name. He mentioned the name Franklin in passing, but it didn't register with me."

"You'll want to see this," said the old man, retrieving a century-old photo of a man in uniform. "When my Great-granddad was in the First Alabama, they were General Sherman's bodyguard when they visited here. He knew he couldn't go home and liked the area so much, he relocated here after the war with a bunch of other men from the same area. Some of the men were from their squad at the LaGrange Military Academy. Everyone had come to refer to Grandpa Ridge by the name Franklin, so he never changed it."

"Just like John Paul left his last name as Jones after the war because that's how everybody knew him," added a triumphant Hannah.

"Yes," continued the old man. "Ridge and my grandmother had three children—Jeremiah, Margaret, and Ulysses. That was my grandfather, who then had James, who then had me. We turned the farmhouse into a bed and breakfast."

Hannah looked at a picture of the young man in an officer's uniform.

"Do you know what happened to Caleb?" asked Hannah. "I assume he switched sides, or at least supported something other than the Confederate Army, but I don't know how."

"I know Grandpa Ridge had a pen pal in Bermuda that he wrote letters to with the name Franklin. But nobody in the family kept the letters," replied the man.

Hannah stayed the night, hearing family stories and reveling in their memories. They called other relatives, who came to meet Hannah and hear her stories from the journal. She promised to come back so they could meet Earl and Lisa. Hopefully on her next visit, she'd bring a male friend as well.

But for now, she had to make a detour to a ten-mile strip of land that just happened to be in the middle of the ocean.

Chapter 36
Den of Spies and Scalawags

Hanna, Mike, Earl, and Lisa got off the water taxi at St. George's Town, Bermuda. They stared at the two-story, old Globe Hotel. Had it not been for the mustard-gold-painted stucco and large Bermuda shutters, it might have passed for a large American home in an affluent suburb. They picked the town and hotel after talking to some Bermuda residents who said it was the center of things during the American Civil War. One person thought there were even some Franklins *and* Rochesters in the area.

"It's hard to imagine that this was the Civil War's version of Casablanca with spies, ship captains, and shady merchants trying to find passage for illegal cargo to supply the Confederate Army," said Hannah.

As they stood, a couple locals skirted past what they took to be tourists. As luck would have it, the hotel was now the Bermuda National Trust Museum. The building seemed to be empty as the four quietly walked through the museum, reading each exhibit featuring model ships and references to Bermuda's illustrious past as a hotbed of spies and scalawags. There was no reference to Caleb, as they feared.

They were about to leave when Hannah saw an old man sitting behind the gift shop counter.

"Excuse me, sir," she said pensively, "I know this is strange, but we're looking for a man who may have worked in this town to help the American Civil War effort named Caleb Franklin or Caleb Rochester. Have you ever heard of either of those names?"

The old man coughed. "Not in relation to the war exactly. I'm more familiar with that family name in reference to the yellow fever epidemic."

"When was that?" asked Hannah.

"That happened at the close of the Civil War in 1864, when some sailors with the disease came to port. The fever swept through the island, infecting virtually every resident and killing hundreds. Back in those days, there was no real treatment. Luckily, a young pharmacist came here who wasn't inclined to fight for the Union or the Confederacy. He was more humanitarian-minded and supplied medicine to either side of the war at a low cost. He was here when the yellow fever epidemic swept the island. He was a consummate reader who found some reference to a Cuban doctor who was the first to link yellow fever to mosquitoes. He somehow got hold of insect netting and made it part of the treatment and prevention. He saved the island."

"Where did he live?" asked Earl when the old man's silence seemed to indicate the story was over.

"I don't rightly know," the old man shrugged. "You can go to the Franklin Family Pharmacy and ask them. They might know. It's right up the street."

It was dusk as the four ran to the little shop to get there before closing. They approached as a woman was reaching for the closed sign. "Can I help you folks with a prescription?"

Hanna almost didn't know where to start. "No. I know this may sound strange, but we're looking for an Alabama man who might have come here during the Civil War named Caleb, Franklin, or Rochester."

"He might have been married to a woman named Millie," quickly added Earl.

The woman was silent, then smiled and pointed to a Civil War-era black-and-white photo on the wall behind the counter. "You mean my great grandfather and grandmother."

"Well, what do you know? He was buried facing blue. Just as he predicted," smiled Earl.

The four enjoyed several days with the extended Rochester and Franklin families, now numbering over one hundred, who came from all over the island to view the journal and hear about their adventure. The Franklin branch explained that Caleb and Millie took the Franklin name hoping to eventually return to Alabama. In the event the Confederacy won the war, Caleb would avoid arrest for fleeing conscription. But by war's end, Caleb and Millie had come to love Bermuda and were widely known by the Franklin name, so they kept it. The Rochesters and Franklins knew they were one in the same, but never discussed it with locals. After two days, Hannah and Mike slipped out to a beach hotel to explore each other, while Earl and Lisa took up the narrative. Before they left, Hannah called Bert at the Leigh Acres Library, who agreed to indefinitely loan the journal to the Rochester family on the condition that they get a library card to "check it out proper."

THE END

ABOUT THE AUTHOR

The Wisconsin born author left the world of corporate banking to take a position in a small Alabama town. There he became close friends with his Dixie born neighbors who shared insights into their town's unique role in several national events. This is the first book in a series featuring a sleuth who uncovers local mysteries tied to these pivotal events in US history.

Shawn received his BS and MBA from Marquette University which evolved into a banking career. To fund college, Shawn enlisted as a Petty Officer in the US Coast Guard Reserve where he obtained a love for maritime history. Shawn's first Book, *Rescue at the Top of the World*, recreated a key maritime disaster following two years of research into century old vessel logs and diaries. This work was subsequently featured annually on the History Channel, which led to becoming a maritime lecturer on various US cruise lines.

Shawn still works in banking and currently lives with his wife Margaret in Birmingham, AL. From there, they travel frequently to visit friends in Leighton, AL, where they collect insights for the mystery series.

His cats, Baxter and Lillie, along with the neighbor's dogs, Houdini and Sugar Ray, actively provide material for the series.

Appendix

LaGrange Military Academy

The LaGrange Military Academy (known today as the LaGrange College site) is located on the crest of a mountain outside Leighton, Alabama. LaGrange College was founded in 1829, with enrollment reaching a peak of 139 students in 1845. After encountering serious financial constraints, the college was subsequently moved to Florence, Alabama, where it ultimately became known as the University of North Alabama. However, the move to Florence was controversial, resulting in select students and faculty remaining at the Leighton site and reopening the school as the LaGrange Military Academy. Enrollment subsequently rose to approximately two hundred cadets, whereupon it became known as the "West Point of the South." After the majority of cadets joined the Confederate Army, the few remaining students were mustered into the newly formed 35th Alabama Infantry Regiment. The Academy was summarily closed.

Today the site accepts visitors and contains:

- Plantation Log Kitchen
- Barber Shop
- Black Smith Shop
- Country Store
- Post Office
- Welcome Center/Museum
- Bed & Breakfast Inn
- Barn
- Smoke House
- Wedding Chapel/ School House
- Outhouse (toilet)
- Caretaker's House
- Three storage buildings

- Monument Markers
- Tabernacle
- Observatory

The site does not contain any ruins of the school itself including the walls described in the book. They were inserted for creative license only.

LaGrange College Site Annual Civil War Reenactment

Each year, LaGrange College, the site of the LaGrange Military Academy, holds a Civil War reenactment as their largest annual fundraiser. If you're in the area, feel free to visit and enjoy chicken stew, burgers, and hot dogs. The author, a Yankee, and his neighbor, a lifelong town resident, volunteered as cooks for several consecutive years.

Leigh Acres (fictional)

Leigh Acres is a fictional town with some similarity by geographic location to Leighton, Alabama. Descriptions are likewise based on Helena, Alabama, which is located over two hours from the LaGrange Military Academy site. Any similarity to residents of either town are coincidental.

Winston County, Alabama

Winston County in northern Alabama is very similar in nature to the area presented in the book. The topography is hilly and known for its shallow soil, unsuitable for plantation-style agriculture. As a result, the county contained very few slaves at the time of the Civil War. Area family farmers generally viewed the Confederacy with suspicion, fearing that secession benefited plantation owners at their expense. The

Winston County representative refused to sign Alabama's ordinance of secession, leading to his arrest. On release, he ultimately became a proponent of the Union and spent the duration of the war in prison. Many Winston County residents refused conscription into the Confederate Army and joined the Union. A meeting was held at Looney's Tavern, where a resolution declared that if a state could secede from the Union, then a county could secede from the state.

Winston County suffered from an internal war where Confederate home guardsmen were at odds with Union-leaning families. By war's end, Winston County had been largely devastated by its own people.

After the war, Winston County became a political center for the Republican Party, in contrast to the remainder of the state, which was comprised of Democrats (note that the parties' social and political positions were generally the reverse of today). Winston County attracts tourists who enjoy outdoor dramas surrounding conflict in the Civil War and rides on a passenger boat named the *Free State Lady*. The "Dual Destiny" memorial statue of a young soldier dressed in both Union and Confederate uniform parts is the subject of frequent photographs.

A fact-based musical drama, *Incident at Looney's Tavern*, was written by Lanny McAlister in 1986, and first performed in 1987. It depicts the events in Winston County following the 1861 Alabama Secession Convention in Montgomery. The drama focuses on Christopher Sheats, the Winston County delegate who opposed secession. In 1993, it was named Alabama's Official Outdoor Musical Drama.

1st Alabama Cavalry (Union)

The Union 1st Alabama Cavalry existed and was comprised of recruits from in and around Winston

County, near Huntsville, Alabama. This unit primarily scouted, conducted raids on Confederate positions, guarded the infantry's flanks, and provided screening to the marching infantry.

One of its most notable assignments was to act as escort to Major General William T. Sherman on his march to the sea. The regiment was mustered out of service on October 20, 1865, with only 397 men remaining out of the two thousand original men. Of that number, over three hundred were killed and almost ninety captured.

Caleb, Ridge, and Millie (fictional)

Caleb Rochester, Ridge Sexton, and Millie Swanson are fictional characters created to represent any cadet originating from a northern Alabama County with conflicting sentiments about the secession movement from the Union. Millie represented the prospects of a young, impoverished woman of the times.

Miss Cecelia Stovall and the Stovall Mansion

Cecelia Stovall's mansion, located in Bartow County, Georgia, was officially called Shelman Heights (Stovall's married name). Cecelia Stovall met William Tecumseh Sherman, the West Point roommate of her brother Marcellus. While at a dance, Sherman made his interest known, but was rejected and she reputedly remarked, "Your eyes are so cold and cruel. I pity the man who ever becomes your foe. Ah, how you would crush an enemy." To this, Sherman replied, "Even though you were my enemy, my dear, I would ever love and protect you."

General Sherman happened upon the mansion, which prominently stood high above the Etowah River on Sherman's march to the sea. On arrival, an African American servant who remained after the family fled mentioned that he was glad Miss Cecelia was not there to see the Yankee soldiers looting her home. Upon further examination, General Sherman learned that Miss Cecelia was in fact the object of his former desire. Sherman thereupon ordered that everything taken from the home be returned and guards placed at the house. He also left a message, retained in the family records, that read: "You once said that I would crush an enemy and you pitied my foe. Do you recall my reply? Although many years have passed, my answer is the same. 'I would ever shield and protect you.' That I have done. Forgive all else. I am only a soldier." To the African American servant he added verbally, "Say to your mistress for me that she might have remained in her home in safety; that she and her property would have been protected." The mansion burned in 1911.

Poor Richard's Bed and Breakfast (fictional)
The B&B is fictional based on what could have been created if two members of the 1st Alabama Cavalry had settled at this location rather than return to the devastated Winston County.

John Paul Jones of the Riddle
The references to John Paul Jones in the riddle are historically accurate. A more complete examination of Jones is as follows: John Jones was born along the southwest coast of Scotland and started his maritime career at the age of thirteen as an apprentice. His elder brother William Paul had married and settled in Fredericksburg, Virginia, where Paul visited on several voyages.

Paul sailed aboard a number of British merchant ships, where he rose in the ranks to become first mate on the merchant vessel *Two Friends*. It was his next voyage aboard the vessel *John*, in 1768, that Paul advanced to become captain after both the captain and a ranking mate died of yellow fever. During his second voyage aboard *John* in 1770, Paul had one of his crew flogged for a disciplinary matter who later died. Unfortunately for Paul, the crewman was an adventurer (versus a professional sailor) from an influential Scottish family. Despite the fact that the crewman likely died of yellow fever, Paul was imprisoned, though subsequently released.

Leaving Scotland, Paul took command of the vessel *Betsy* for eighteen months, whereupon Jones was allegedly attacked by a mutinous crewman. In the ensuing sword fight, Jones slew the man. He claimed self-defense, but feared a court conviction due to the influence of the first Scottish family from the prior incident. So, he fled to his brother's home in Fredericksburg, Virginia, leaving his fortune behind.

On his arrival, Paul changed his last name to Jones, becoming known as John Jones (not unlike people today assuming the name John Smith). Some North Carolina historians believe Paul took the name to honor Willie Jones of Halifax, North Carolina. Shortly thereafter, the newly named Jones joined the Patriots in fighting the British at sea. Jones enjoyed success against his former country in a series of commands. In a short period between ships, Jones cemented a close friendship with Benjamin Franklin in Boston, Massachusetts.

After another series of actions against the British, Jones took command of the newly named *Bon Homme Richard*. This ship was so named in honor of his friend Benjamin Franklin, by making reference to the man who penned *Poor Richard's Almanac*. Aboard the *Bon Homme Richard*, Jones was pursued by several royal warships to the English shore when he engaged the HMS *Serapis* off Flamborough Head, East Yorkshire.

Outgunned, Jones made every effort to lock the *Bon Homme Richard* and the *Serapis* together for close action fighting. It was in this action that he reputedly uttered the phrase "I have not yet begun to fight!" in reply to a demand to surrender. Crew members reported that the words actually spoken were more akin to "I may sink, but I'll be damned if I strike." The *Serapis* surrendered to Jones two hours later.

Caleb's Grandfather (fictional)

While Caleb's father was fictional, several Alabama Winston County residents served in the Continental Army during the Revolutionary War. These included:

- Jesse Dodd
- Stephen Garrison
- Andrew Nelson
- Mathey Payne (likely Mathew today)
- Jacob Pruet

Hannah's House

The little white "Cotton Mill Overseer House" does exist in Leighton, Alabama, across from a vacant lot in front of an abandoned cotton mill. The author lived in this house and cut the lawn to stop late-night activities as described in the book. Upon cutting the grass, graffiti was exposed that was likewise painted over by the author and his neighbors. Neighbors likewise maintained a garden for use by anyone in the community.

Colbert County Land Auction and Country House

In 2014, Colbert County, which encompasses Leighton, Alabama, held the largest land auction in the area's memory. The author bid on a country house similar to that described in the book and lost to another bidder who bought the house as part of a large parcel of farm land. As of the writing of this book, the house is still unoccupied.

Venture (aka *Sea Venture*) was part of a 1609 mission to supply the Jamestown Colony. On route, *Venture* was separated from the fleet during a storm and became shipwrecked on the shores of Bermuda. The surviving crew built two new ships from the wreckage: *Deliverance* and *Patience.* The two smaller ships continued to the Jamestown Colony, where they found 60 survivors from the original 500. On return to England, news of their harrowing experience was thought to have inspired the Shakespearean play, *The Tempest.*

Other Union Alabama Regiments

In addition to the 1st Alabama Cavalry Regiment referenced in the book, several other Union regiments were comprised of Alabama residents. It's interesting to note that most of these units were African American.

African American Union Regiments from Alabama:
- 1st Alabama Siege Artillery Regiment; also known as the 7th U.S. Heavy Artillery Regiment
- 1st Alabama Infantry Regiment; also known as the 55th U.S. Infantry Regiment
- 2nd Alabama Infantry Regiment; also known as the 110th U.S. Infantry Regiment
- 3rd Alabama Infantry Regiment; also known as the 111th U.S. Infantry Regiment
- 4th Alabama Infantry Regiment; also known as the 106th U.S. Infantry Regiment

Caucasian Union Regiments from Alabama
- 1st Alabama Cavalry Regiment
- 1st Tennessee & Alabama Independent Vidette Cavalry